The Saga of Doubtful Sound

ALWYN DOW

Dedicated to Barack Obama on his victory for a second term
as US President in November 2012.

Order this book online at www.trafford.com
or email orders@trafford.com

Most Trafford titles are also available at major online book retailers.

Printed in the United States of America.

ISBN: 978-1-4669-6660-4 (sc)
ISBN: 978-1-4669-6661-1 (e)

Library of Congress Control Number: 2012920540

Trafford rev. 11/08/2012

 www.trafford.com

North America & international
toll-free: 1 888 232 4444 (USA & Canada)
phone: 250 383 6864 ♦ fax: 812 355 4082

CONTENTS

Part One 'Didn't He Ramble'   1

Part Two 'Sentimental Journey.'   39

Part Three 'Hurrah For Hollywood.'   69

Part Four 'Hydra'   99

Part Five Reuben's Revenge   113

Synopsis

Jed and Gina are reporters who find themselves caught up in a chain of events linking the world of Jazz with a worldwide racist conspiracy. There is not much time to be romantic but they manage it somehow. Jedsy Lomax worked for the New York Echo. His job included a column called 'Jazz, a Doubtful Sound' that had received International acclaim. You could say that a good news story and jazz were his only true loves apart from a Tuscan beauty called Gina. Stories came and went but even he was surprised at the twists and turns that would follow an obituary that he read in the newspaper in 1942, a story that would re-emerge decade after decade through the jazz world of the Solidar family and lead to the exposure of a white supremacist group called 'Hydra'

A DOUBTFUL SOUND

PART ONE. (Didn't he ramble. 1900-42—REUBEN SOLIDAR)

An obituary in the paper interested Jed in the career of one Reuben Solidar, a jazz musician of some note. He quickly obtained an interview with Reuben's brother Cecil, and uncovered some very sinister revelations in a 'jazz age' where organised crime and racism were uneasy bedfellows with Jelly Roll Morton, King Oliver, 'Satchmo' and others.

PART TWO. (Sentimental Journey. 1943-53—CECIL SOLIDAR)

Reuben was given a posthumous award from the NAACP, and this was passed—on to Jed by Cecil, with an appeal that he would seek justice for his brother. It seemed natural therefore that he would now follow Cecil's work with bands of the 'Big Band' era such as Dorsey and Herman, as he tried to track down those responsible, and much more besides.

PART THREE. (Hurrah for Hollywood. 1954-64—REUBEN JUNIOR)

In 1963 the death of Marilyn Monroe shocked Hollywood and the world. Rumours were rife about the role of the Mafia and even the President. A week later Jed received a call from Cecil's son, Reuben Junior, a very promising trumpeter with Stan Kenton, who had been arrested on suspicion of her murder following rumours of an affair. He admitted that he had been an informer to a racist group but Jed agreed to hear his story. Finally, he thought, he might get to the bottom of a puzzle that had eluded him for decades. Reuben began in 1954 with a girl called Kim Novak.

PART FOUR. (Hydra. 1770-1870)

We gain insight into Hydra's origins.

PART FIVE. (Reuben's Revenge 1964)

Reuben is in trouble again when his tour of the Deep South with 'Muddy' Waters seems to implicate him in the murder of Civil Rights activists in Tennessee, but paradoxically this will lead Jed and Gina to the Hydra's lair in 'Doubtful Sound' NZ.

(Synopses, timelines and appendices are after Parts 1, 2 & 3. Characters in this story will not converse in the vernacular to any marked degree. There would be too many pitfalls to beware of in that approach.)

PART ONE
'DIDN'T HE RAMBLE'

Reuben Solidar was dead. Naturally, being somewhat of a 'bit' musician this was hardly news in the grand scheme of things. However, there were some details in his obituary in 1942 that intrigued reporter Jed Lomax.

Firstly, why would he be killed during a Japanese-American race clash 3 months after Pearl Harbour? Secondly why was he involved in Japanese-American affairs at all and thirdly, why was he known as 'The Ghost'? Jed was a reporter and his nose sensed a story, but he did not expect to put his life in danger, nor to end up on the other side of the world as he and Gina tracked down a group called 'Hydra.'

Jedsy Lomax considered himself to be the luckiest man alive. Almost by chance (and with the help of a friend) he had landed a job at a New York newspaper, and, not only that, he was soon appointed to the arts desk that included music. Here he was able to indulge his love of Jazz with topical news stories and the occasional scandal. His regular weekly column entitled 'Jazz, A Doubtful Sound' had won many awards in the US.

True he could be lonely at times because he didn't have a wife but he often had a 'lady friend' for company and there was always his collection of Jazz records to listen to. Louis in the morning, Bill Evans for a romantic dinner, then Django on the terrace followed by Billie Holliday who might accompany the sounds of love into the night.

It was now 8am and he was running late when, just as he was finishing his shave he became aware of a movement behind him causing him to glance once more into his mirror and there she was, slightly crumpled after last night; 'But Beautiful,' he hummed. This was Gina and she was wearing a white towelling robe and a lovely smile. He didn't turn around but kept his gaze firmly on the mirror as she came closer, gently loosening the towel robe as she did so. The mirror steamed and he had to wipe it clear. Now she was naked and it was Jed that was steaming. 'Oh no!' he cried out, 'you can't get me like that. I've got a meeting in 20 minutes.' Still she advanced and manoeuvred herself past him, tips touching tips for a brief moment.

'Well, you wouldn't want to be late now would you?' she said as she stepped inside the shower cubicle and shut the door. Jed was left alone with a mirror and a razor. Small comfort.

For the next few moments he made coffee and toast whist reading the newspaper. He liked having Gina there although their 'love affair' was quite new. He liked to make a fuss of her and because she loved honey it always had to be on the table at breakfast. Funny though, have you noticed how a honey jar remains somewhat sticky no matter how many times you wash it? And have you tried turning the pages of a newspaper with 'tacky' hands? This was a problem for Jed as all the pages seemed to stick and the more he tried to separate them, the worse it got. He was in a bit of a mess and he was about to call her when she strolled in from the bathroom and quickly took charge by dividing up the sections of the newspaper before placing her little finger in the honey jar and offering it to Jed on his lips with a smile. 'I shan't be going in until later. We've got meetings up until six so we'll start after lunch I think. So, what's in the news?' she said. 'Come and un-stick me and I'll tell you,' laughed Jed who still could not disentangle himself from the Business pages. She did, but not without the loss of half the Sports page as they struggled with the paper and the honey jar.

'Right, let's see, here we are then, April 10th 1942.' he said, 'There's more about the war and a big article about the internments. Here.' he said, handing those pages over, 'that's your baby isn't it?' She was a news reporter on the paper with an interest in social affairs so she thanked him and began to read, whilst negotiating the mischievous honey jar and the paper. She had slightly more success than Jed, it must be admitted. He browsed through what was left of the sports pages and then turned his attention to the obituaries. He often did this, hoping to latch on to a good story or even some malicious gossip. It all made good news and there was usually a scandal or two in the Arts.

However, it was a small obituary tucked away that caught his eye. It said,

'<u>Reuben Solidar (1900-42)</u> It has been reported that Solidar was killed during recent race clashes in Los Angeles following Japanese-American internments. The police have issued a statement saying that he, and another, had been found on the beach and both had been shot. Solidar was a jazz saxophonist who had worked in the Big Bands quite recently and had become known as 'The Ghost.' He started his career in New Orleans in the 1920's with his twin brother Cecil who still lives in New York. A more detailed obit will follow.'

Jed felt sad. He had followed and respected the work of Reuben especially since he had become aware of the horrific accident that had nearly cost him his life. Jed was sad but he was also puzzled. He called over to Gina, 'Says here that Reuben Solidar was killed in LA race clash. Does it say anything about violence during the internments?' 'No.' she replied, 'seems to be rather peaceful although it does mention some scuffles in this article. Why?' 'It says Reuben was murdered, not injured in a scuffle,' he said, 'would you pass that article over if you've finished please?' She did so straight away saying, 'There you are. It all seems a bit unfair for the poor Japanese families, but I can't see anything about murder. You read it and I'll make some more coffee.' Jed picked the paper up and began to read and this is what it said.

'Under Executive Order 9066 more Japanese Americans are being removed from their homes in California. This is a Federal Order from the President, in other words the matter has not been left to the Governor. No doubt there had been contingency plans since Pearl Harbour but as the perceived threat has widened, it seems that the government has decided to take Draconian measures. As recently as January Singapore has been captured, following the loss of Wake Island and Hong Kong in December. It seems that all Japanese Americans are deemed to be potential spies or saboteurs so Internment camps have been set up with the main one at Tule Lake. Other locations have been made available many hundreds of miles from the coast where they might start a new life.'

Jed put the paper down with a puzzled frown. He was trying to work out why Reuben had been in LA and caught up in some trouble. He looked back at the brief obituary sensing that there was a story there, somewhere.

Now we know that Jed was a bit of a Jazz enthusiast, and he got a feeling that this was not an adequate testimony to the life of Reuben who, it was alleged in some quarters, had indeed been involved in many recordings of note. The trouble was that, since his disfiguring accident, he had not played in public again. Some said however that he had been the musician of choice 'off stage' when bandleaders looked for a 'gold standard' performance, earning him the sobriquet 'The Ghost' (as in a ghost writer). Some alleged that he had created the Glenn Miller 'sound' in which the clarinet took the trumpet lead, and that he had tried this out with Fletcher Henderson two years before. Anyhow, Jed thought he deserved more than a five line obituary, and he was determined to find out how much of all this was really true. He decided that he would track Cecil down to find out, but he wasn't prepared for what followed, as his story took him into the shady world of politics, crime starting with a shadowy group called the 'ALL'.

(Authors note *The American Liberty League was founded in 1934.*)

Gina sat patiently and gave him a big smile. When they had met three months ago, he said that the name 'Gina' must mean 'Smile' in some foreign, tribal or space creature language. She just called him 'Jed', sometimes adding 'Are you ready for bed?' They had laughed so easily and loved so lovingly in such a short time, that it seemed natural for him to want to share his thoughts. She was not a 'Jazz buff' like Jed but she was intrigued. 'Do you mean that they just used him behind the scenes?'

she asked. 'I don't know about that' he replied, 'I suppose he got well paid, or maybe he only got union rates.' Gina looked at him sternly, 'Well Mr Lomax', she called him that when she wanted to be taken seriously, 'you'd better find out hadn't you? You've been saying how you'd like a change, now here's you chance to make something of yourself as a writer. Give those editors your notice tomorrow.' Jed was taken aback but said that he'd think about it, 'Damn the girl, she's done it again.' he thought 'She thinks what I'm thinking before I think it.'

And that's how the story of Reuben Solidar began to be told, and how, in the telling of it, the unscrupulous world of the ALL was exposed, but unfortunately not stopped, as it flitted anonymously, sometimes as agent and sometimes as intermediary, for groups with similar agendas. Initially it had chosen to operate with complete anonymity but when it became apparent that fear could be more of a powerful persuader than action, they began to leave 'calling cards,' usually 'ALL' graffiti as proof of their involvement in some crime or another. It was alleged furthermore that they had links with agencies of organised crime, as well as formal political parties. Some said that they were an 'Underground KKK' as that group began to lose influence, others that there was a another group headed by a 'Top Man', known only as 'The Chief' from the world of politics and business who pulled the strings and paid the bills.

Like a Hydra perhaps, the beast that grew two heads when one was destroyed, or like an Onion, with layers, gradually exposing a long awaited 'Leader'. As Reuben had got close to this shadowy figure, his life had become extremely dangerous and if Jed followed his tracks, his would be too. Perhaps if Gina had known that Jed's interest in Reuben Solidar would uncover not one, but a series of conspiracies she might have stopped him there and then, but perhaps not, because, after all her job for many years had been to report on the 'Affairs of the Nation.' She was not to know at this early stage that he was entering a world where some people would stop at nothing, including murder, to keep a secret. They would soon find out however that, not only his life but hers also, would be under threat. For now, he just wanted to find Cecil and they were not thinking of any danger. 'Will it be OK if I come along?' she asked, 'You never know, I might even be useful.' Jed smiled. He didn't like to be pinned down but this seemed like too good an offer to turn away, and anyway there might be some 'fringe benefits' he thought rather optimistically. 'Be my guest' he said, giving her a hug.

Gina

Gina Lombardi was in her early twenties and she didn't quite know how she had found herself alongside Jed at this time. They were very different to look at it's true she tall, dark and shapely and he, well she would say, 'Round em up cowboy.' that being an affectionate reference to his similarity to Alan Ladd the Hollywood movie star, as well as a tease.

No matter, there was something about him, she thought, something of the restless explorer, always digging and delving into this or that story until 'The pips squeaked.' In that respect she was much the same but her interest lay in politics and social affairs due in no small part to her family's hurried exit from Italy in 1924. She was only a baby at the time but her father told her later about the murder of Matteotti the Prime Minister allegedly by Mussolini's Black Shirts. It was then that he had fully understood the brutality of the Fascists and, being a socialist himself, he decided it was time to flee with his wife and his two little twin girls, Gina and Marie. He was a doctor so it wasn't too hard for him to find work in New York, while Mama stayed at home initially to look after Gina and her sister then she worked at the local hospital as a nurse.

The events in Italy were always a topic of conversation when Gina was growing up, so much so that when she went to University she joined the 'Young Communists' to raise funds for the opposition parties there. Soon after this her parents told her and Marie that they were actually going to go back to Italy to help the partisans in their fight against the Fascists, and then Marie decided to join them. Gina was heartbroken and above all she was fearful for their safety but they persuaded her to stay in New York. She continued her protest activities but this was not too easy when she got a job at the New York Herald. It was here that she met Jed and he was immediately struck, not only by her beauty but also by her forthright and passionate nature. She was emotional and he liked that too. When she cared about something or someone they knew it, and how. Gina cared about Jed and it was one of the reasons that he always felt lucky.

In 1942 the Italian forces were fighting in North Africa but in Rome the Fascists had begun Jewish deportations and Gina felt helpless. She joined the Italian-Jewish Alliance, a non sectarian group, it being understood that many high officials in the Roman Catholic establishment did very little to help at this time. 'Don't make matters worse,' seemed to be their byword. However there is no doubt that many Catholics, Protestants and others did belong to the I JA. This took up much of Gina's time, but now it seemed, Jed had a mystery on his hands and she wanted to help.

1900-32 'Mr Jelly Roll' and a 'Gig for Zig'

They took an overnight trip to New Orleans and soon found Cecil living quite comfortably just off Canal St. Over coffee and bourbon, and more bourbon, he began to tell them Reuben's story, which to some extent was his own as well. Before he began though, he said that he had a very important statement to make and that there would be little point in talking to them unless they made him a promise. Naturally they agreed and waited for him to begin.'I want you to find out whether Reuben's death was an accident.' he said. 'I do know that he went to LA to help Billy Shu's family who were about to be interned as Japanese aliens even though his mum was born in the States. Reuben and Billy were close ever since they were in the Henderson band. I spoke to Billy and he just told me that he had lost Reuben in a crowd that was protesting and that the police found him later. Billy thinks there's more to it and so do I, so I haven't released the body for burial yet. Will you help?'

They both nodded and Jed said, 'I'm sure that we'll do all we can to get to the bottom of this. We'll get in touch with Billy and get down there. You can rely on me but we'll need some background. Now for a start will it be OK if we record all this to get all the details straight? We'd like to do an article as well as an obituary about Reuben, so we need to go back to the beginning, back to New Orleans at the turn of the century. What was it really like, and are the stories about Glenn Miller true?'

Cecil agreed and, as he still had his trombone on a stand in the corner of the room, he picked it up with a flourish as if to seal the agreement like an Indian peace pipe, asking them, 'Now do you recognize this one? (He obviously missed playing). Jed was quick to respond after this musical introduction. 'Ory's Creole Trombone!' he stated with some sense of satisfaction, and with no question mark because he knew that he was right. 'Correct' said Cecil, 'Now, that's a good a place to start as any isn't it? So firstly I'll tell you about funerals, parades, Freddy Keppard, Kid Ory and the New Orleans Creole community'

Jed and Gina sat back and listened as he began his story.

Cecil's story in his words. New Orleans 1912

Aunt Jenny died in 1912 when we were twelve, Reuben and me, and Papa told us we must go to the funeral and follow the band as they played 'Didn't he ramble' and other tunes, first as a dirge and then into a speeded up happy sound as 'The Saints went marching in.' (to Heaven of course). It was my first sight of a trombone and I knew that I wanted to play it one day. I didn't know it at the time but the trombonist on that occasion was none other than Edward 'Kid' Ory, who had just arrived in New Orleans from La Place, Louisiana where he was born.

As for the word 'Creole' well, people in our neighbourhood paid little attention to racial stereotypes in those days, because just about everyone we knew was of mixed parentage or descent, ourselves included. The general term used in Louisiana was 'Creole,' but that covered many mixes of different races including Negro, Hispanic and European.

Authors note *(The largest singular group in New Orleans were the French, still 25% in 1902, after the Louisiana Purchase of 1803 when they had sold the territory to the new USA.)*

Many 'mixed race' or 'black' bands in the early years included the word 'Creole' in the name of the band, including King Oliver, whereas the 'white' bands of the era, (such as the ODJB-The Original Dixieland Jass Band) often adopted the term 'Dixieland.' or 'Dixie.'

Authors note *(Dixie was a term that described the Southern 'Slave States' of the Civil War. It was also a New Orleans 10 Dollar Bill, the 'DIX'.)*

As I said, no one asked questions back then and, for our part that's just the way it was. Papa was actually half Cuban and Mama half French so we tended to be accepted in any company locally, except you wouldn't want to venture too far up river on your own. Some white folks just hated the Blacks and things haven't changed to this day I can tell you.

(Jed interjected here with a question. 'But doesn't your profession, as a musician, give you some kind of status, a kind of importance.' he asked.)

Not at all (Cecil continued) the only place we got any consideration as black musicians (apart from some appreciation in some bands) was in Europe where, even in Germany under the Nazis, many people valued our work. In the States as you know the old divisions of the Civil War lingered on in the South, and in New York, Harlem was virtually a ghetto.

We lived in the Algiers District in New Orleans and I suppose that we were quite well off compared to some, because Papa always had regular work as a barber and Mama was a seamstress. In fact that's how our musical education began because they both worked for a firm called 'Spikes and Morton' in downtown Canal Street. We used to go and sit in the Hairdressers chairs after school and that's how we met Mr Morton.

His splendid name was 'Ferdinand Lemott Morton' to be precise. We found out that he was a 'hustler' of extraordinary versatility with interests in a club hotel, (with his wife Anita) cabarets, music, dance halls, gambling and, a new word for us, pimping. Nevertheless he took a great interest in our musical development and he was a very, very strict teacher. We didn't mind, because we had found out by then that we were in the hands of one of the pre-eminent musicians in town, namely 'Mr Jelly Roll Morton.' He told us that he had been playing piano in Storyville brothels since about 1906 and we couldn't wait to join him! No chance of that for a while though. Meanwhile he had big plans to form a band and go to Chicago, which was 'every musicians dream.' he said.

New Orleans is known for 'Mardis Gras' of course, and the local jazz bands celebrated along with the rest of the town. Foremost for many years was the legendary

Buddy Bolden, about whom stories are legion. He held sway at Pete Lala's Cabaret Club for many years, and it was said that he was such a powerful player that his sound could be heard many blocks away. He did not record, some thought, because he did not want to be copied, but in fact he was ill and off the scene by 1906, which is well before the earliest recorded 'Jass' of the ODJB in 1917. Joe 'King' Oliver was there as well with a wonderful band by 1921 including Honore Dutrey and Johnny Dodds plus the saxophone of David Jones. Reuben would listen to him for hours.

Jazzmen love Mardis Gras but it was around long before us. Some say from the 1870's when the Russian Grand Duke Alexis gave it official colours, Purple for Justice, Gold for Power, and Green for Faith. I don't know about that. I bet similar celebrations have been held since Domesday! Mardis Gras means 'Fat Tuesday' and it's the day before Ash Wednesday. In other words it's a time to let your hair down before a period of calm and reflection over Easter. So a kind of surreal madness is allowed to prevail on the streets for a time. This is led by groups known as 'krews' such as the mystic krew of Comus, the Elves of Oberon, the High Priests of Mithras and others. They dress as man beasts, demi beasts or apes and toss 'throws' into the crowd, sometimes beads and sometimes coins or toys. All good clean fun I assure you although it can seem sinister at times especially if you have a nervous disposition.

(Gina spoke up here remembering that she had been to a Mardis Gras when she was nine and was scared out of her life. 'In fact,' she said, 'I don't think I could go again without having nightmares.' Cecil smiled and said that it was a bit scary but quite harmless, and continued.)

Reuben and me, we always played along with the procession and most of the musicians we knew did also. New Orleans buzzed with music in those days, even though the infamous Storyville (Red Light) District closed down in 1917. There was plenty of work around in bars, 'rent parties', weddings, funerals and the River Boats on the Missisippi of course. You'd have thought that this was an ideal environment but it wasn't.

In 1905 Yellow Fever had struck and carried our dear Mama away with hundreds of others. The streets were full of moaning trombones and mournful trumpets for weeks as we buried our dead. In 1909 and 1915 there were destructive hurricanes and we were busy again. As you probably know, much of New Orleans is below sea level so we have a system of barriers (the levees) that are supposed to keep the sea out. Doesn't always work though especially after a Hurricane. The area is known as 'the swamp' and it's surrounded by cypress groves called the 'backwoods' where we always played as kids without any fear of danger until the warnings sounded.

In New Orleans many of our problems were associated with the weather and disease but elsewhere political and industrial unrest were growing with race riots in Chicago and anonymous parcel bombs posted to important figures. These were thought to be the work of the IWW (The International Workers Group), linked to the

'Red Scare' that took hold after the Russian Revolution. A bomb exploded in Wall Street killing 38 people in 1920 and eventually IWW members were executed.

Authors note. *References to these groups are from historical sources.*

I was made much more aware of these events by Reuben who, by then had joined the NAACP and they saw it as their duty to stand solid with the underprivileged workers of the IWW.

On top of all this, there was the ever—present fear of a 'lynching' if us 'black folks' as much smiled at a white girl. It was worse in the countryside, so we mostly stayed in town and travelled north on the Riverboats where it was safer. In some ways racial attacks were getting worse with a new 'Second' Ku Klax Klan formed in 1915. I don't think anyone knows how many died hanging as 'Strange Fruit' (The title of song by Billie Holiday) but they made a count for the year of 1920 and it was seventy, yes, 70 'lynchings' in that second year after the war, when Negroes and Creoles had served just as 'Whitey' had. I'll say more about the war in a minute, but that was the year that changed Reuben. Three of his very best friends, two of them musicians, were found hanging outside Baton Rouge and he confronted me as we headed off for a gig. 'What should we do Bro', what should we do, we must do something mustn't we?' This was a question to me, the senior brother because he always expected me to take the lead in such serious matters. I'm afraid I let him down rather because I reminded him that 'Jim Crow' had been around for a very long time and there was nothing to be done except get on with our lives. He had looked at me with extreme disappointment and such disdain, that I almost curled up in shame. I was stung, 'Well what do you suggest?' I asked him, 'How about we join the Musicians union, that might help.' Once more he gave me that look, as if it was my last chance to redeem myself on this earth. The chance would never come again, not in his eyes anyway. 'Well, don't tell everyone but I'm going to join the NAACP as soon as possible. What do you think about that?' I was shocked I can tell you and I tried everything to get him to change his mind. We never talked of it again until much later when I found out about his activities as a member. Me. I just joined the Union and looked out for work wherever it might take us. I have to admit now though that he was right. The KKK was getting stronger with their defeat of the Oklahoma Governor and they even put up a (Democratic) candidate for President.

But as I said, the war came along and decimated our neighbourhood as men were called up in 'The Draft'. Many of our friends didn't come back, most dying from the outbreak of influenza that was rife. I was exempt because of my bad eyesight and Reuben was sent for training in the military band. It was all over before he was set to go abroad so once more we set about looking for opportunities, and that meant Chicago.

*   *   *   *

Jed decided that it was time for a break before Cecil told them about Chicago so he suggested that they went out for a meal at 'La Trattoria' that was one of his favourite restaurants. Gina was keen but Jed noticed that Cecil was hesitant and asked why, 'There's no problem about colour there I know because I've dined there often and seen every colour of the rainbow.' he said. Cecil smiled. 'No it's not that. It's the ownership. Everyone knows that the Fagiolis, who own the place, are 'in bed' with the Gambini 'family,' in fact it's also known that Mafia meetings are held there regularly and the FBI have bugged the place in the past. I just wouldn't feel comfortable at tables that have been responsible for so much bloodshed, perhaps even Reuben's and anyway, I'm bound to be recognised as his brother and he certainly had enemies here.' Jed was a bit disappointed but above all he was surprised that he himself was so ignorant of the 'legitimate' role played by the Mafia on the streets.

Gina saved the day, 'You know not every Italian is a gangster, I can't speak for the Sicilians mind,' she said with a laugh, 'How about Chok Wongs? You might get the Triads but no Mafia I think.' And so Choks it was with as much as you could eat for 'Nine Dollar' and a free Rice Wine. By now Cecil was keen to start again in Chicago 1923.

Cecil continues his story. Chicago 1923

The biggest thing that got the musicians and others moving north to Chicago was work in the Stockyards or elsewhere. They travelled mostly on the Rock Island and Pacific railway, but when it was our turn we went by Paddle Steamship. This is because we could work our passage in bands such as that of Fate Marable who employed the very best musicians (On the SS Sydney and other vessels) such as Louis Armstrong, Johnny and Baby Dodds, Joe Howard, Johnny St Cyr and others. It was in that band that we got to know Louis, and when he went to Chicago in 1923 to join Joe 'The King' (Oliver), he invited us along as spare musicians, security guards, and bag carriers of course. It was a great opportunity and it introduced us to a life we had only dreamt about, a life of music.

But I'm getting a bit ahead of myself here because the War affected nearly ever family we knew as I said earlier. In 1917 the Government passed the 'Selective Service Act' known by us as the 'Draft.' Many of our friends went to fight in Europe and not many came home. Casualties were high but the worst thing was the influenza epidemic, which accounted for nearly half of all deaths. The US regiments were segregated, but were all known as the 'Dough Boys', possibly because of the shape of the infantry button, I've been told. Reuben and me got our papers as expected, but

I had poor eyesight and was rejected. Reuben was sent for training in the Military Band, but it was all over before they could send him overseas.(He tended to repeat himself sometimes)

We kept going with band work here and there, and in 1923 we got our big break to go with Louis to Chicago. It was said at the time that, although Joe Oliver admired Armstrong, his reason for the invitation was to keep an eye on a potential 'rival.' However, as it turned out they are remembered and valued for quite different contributions to Jazz. Actually it was clear that Oliver was past his best as a trumpet soloist by then, and that his unique gift was in organizing this very special band to make the legendary 1923 Okeh recordings. Louis meanwhile went on to become the 'Great Satchmo' and to record his Hot 5's and 7's.

Apart from that Okeh session, where Reuben and me just watched in awe, there was quite a lot of music around in Chicago for us to take part in but it was no picnic. It was the first year of Prohibition and gangsters such as Al Capone controlled all the 'speakeasies' selling 'bootleg' (illegal) liquor. It was not unusual for the Police to raid a club and tell us to keep playing while a gunfight took place. So when we heard that Louis had got a job in New York to join the excellent Fletcher Henderson Band in 1924 we volunteered to 'carry the bags' again.

(Here Cecil paused so Jed decided that they all needed a rest and, leaving Cecil to his memories they took a taxi back to Jed's flat.)

'Tell the driver to take me home.' Gina said when they arrived, 'I need a good night's rest and your flat isn't the best place for that is it?' She smiled as she held his hand but he could tell that she meant it. 'I'm the one to give the brush off if anyone is,' he muttered to himself but his words said, 'Yes I'm a bit bushed as well. You get a good night and I'll see you soon.' That was ambiguous enough, he thought for her to be kept guessing, but her reply took him by surprise. 'Well I'm planning to visit an old friend soon so it might as well be now.' she said, 'I'll give you a ring when I get back.' With that she pecked him on the cheek and pushed him out of the Cab door. 'Don't forget to pay.' she said as he stood on the pavement in the drizzle. He felt in his pocket and paid the driver in, it must be admitted, a rather irritated manner, and then he climbed up the steps to his flat without waving goodbye.

'Damn it, damn it all.' he said out loud to the boxes that contained his flat keys. 'Drat and Damnation, I think I'm falling in love.' Not surprisingly he did give Gina a ring the next morning, and unsurprisingly she was at home, and quite naturally they agreed to meet at Cecil's later that day as if nothing had happened; but they both knew that a lot had happened as they had sparred for those few moments in the rain.

Jed

As we noted earlier Jed was short and stocky with a breath of country fresh air about him. A Wild West character if ever there was one but it wasn't the Frontier that interested him. Somehow or other he had got a taste for books from a very early age and this had led him to read drama stories of all kinds from Mark Twain to Dickens, but his favourite of all time was Scott FitzGerald with his tales of love, lust and corruption in the 'Jazz Age' and especially 'The Great Gatsby,' a true to life character he thought. Partly as a result of this he found himself working for the Chicago Tribune in the late 30's until his move to New York. Dad had been an architect in Boston and it was here that Jed grew up. However the Great Depression hit the construction business hard and, as building and design contracts fell by over 90%, he became one of the long queues of the unemployed. Later on the family moved to Detroit where he became a supervisor in the Engine Plant at the Ford Motor Company. Jed had been somewhat chastened and a little wary of life after these tough beginnings but he remained an optimist in the true 'Gatsby' tradition. Along with this he had a very tender side probably inherited from his mum 'Rosie' who managed their frugal times without complaint and always with a loving smile. Perhaps it was these lessons that enabled Jed to bounce back so rapidly when he too was laid off from the Tribune.

'Back in the saddle lad,' his Dad would say euphemistically but Jed took the advice seriously and headed for New York. Strangely it was this change of fortune that led him into a new and wonderful 'Jazz Age' right there in the 'Big Apple.' Soon he was working for the New York Times and soon after had his own music programme that he called, 'A Doubtful Sound,' hinting at the precarious questing nature of Jazz. He was made.

Cecil carries on with his story. New York 1924-6

We had hardly arrived in New York before Reuben told me that he had a 'business' to attend to that shouldn't take more than a few weeks. I knew better than to ask too many questions because he could get rather touchy and secretive. Anyway he left and I didn't see him again until the 10th November and I must say he was looking a bit down. He confided that he had been in Wisconsin to support Robert Lafollette's Progressive Party in the General Election. The PP shared many of the aims of the NAACP so Reuben and his colleagues were called out to help. He told me that they had won in Wisconsin but had taken hardly any votes elsewhere and the Republican Calvin Coolidge had become President in a landslide.

Authors note *(The electors rejected Nationalisation and Civil Rights.*

At this point Jed thought that he should make a point or two about Jazz and the political situation that Reuben had got involved in. 'Tell me Cecil,' he said, 'What was it about Reuben that caused him to be so active in causes that seemed to be only vaguely related to issues about black musicians in jazz bands?' Cecil smiled as if to say, 'that's a daft question' but, being a very polite Creole from New Orleans, his reply was courteous in the extreme. 'Reuben was committed to Truth, Fairness and Justice,' he said, 'so am I, but I do nothing about it. So are you and Gina probably but what do you do except fight little battles here and there. That's what nearly everybody does, and it's even worse than that because we collaborate most of the time. It's just another day, another injustice maybe but there's always tomorrow. Reuben didn't need a reason but if there was one it was those fiery crosses of the Ku Klax Klan and the bodies of hanged Negroes, 'Strange Fruit' on the trees. He seemed to understand that the perpetrators of such crimes were given licence in the political sphere and so the battle must be fought there.' Jed felt quite chastened and looked at Gina rather sheepishly. 'I think he's got us there don't you?' he said. 'Yes I agree,' she replied, 'but it's never too late to heed a wake up call. I hope I'll get a chance to do some good before I'm finished.' Jed smiled at her in a rather tender, almost loving way and turned to Cecil. 'There you are, two volunteers for the cause.' he said.

Cecil smiled approvingly, 'Yes, me too. I could have done a lot more you know but there's always got to be a start and this could be it. Now let me get on with the next part of the story before I forget the details . . . .

Fortunately Reuben didn't have much time to lick his political wounds before he got a chance of a lifetime to join the Big Time with Fletcher Henderson. This was a bigger and much more sophisticated band than he was used to. Fletcher Henderson was already a well known pianist and MD when in 1924, he secured a residency at the Roseland ballroom in New York. He had a star-studded band including Charlie Green, (Trombone Cholly of Bessie Smith fame) Coleman Hawkins, Buster Bailey, Don Redman and others, but some flash of inspiration caused Henderson to tempt Louis Armstrong from Chicago. Louis didn't stay long, but once more his records became accepted as masterpieces.

Until Louis' arrival Henderson tended to be lead more of a dance band, playing the 'fox trot' that was all the rage then. But, even after Louis had left, he stuck to this Jazz policy with new stars such as Joe Smith, and even arranged for Benny Goodman in later years. These arrangements could be complex as Pee Wee Russell (The Chicago clarinettist) found out when auditioning for the band. 'Five and Six flats ain't easy for Sax.' he is reputed to have said, turning down the job. It was <u>14 Nov 1924</u>.

Now this was how Reuben got his first big solo break. Coleman Hawkins had been taken ill just before the band were due to record an arrangement for 'Naughty Man' which also included a solo for C melody sax. Apparently Fletcher looked round in despair until Louis said, 'I know someone you could use. Why don't you send for the Ghost? Reuben Solidar is the best 'dep' in town and he can read music 'eyes shut!'

A strange mixture of metaphors you might think, but it convinced Henderson, and Reuben took 'The Hawks' place on the recording. 'The Ghost' was born. Of course they couldn't put his name on the label because of contractual reasons but you can tell it's him. I've got an old 78 here. Just give this a listen. You can tell it's him can't you?' he repeated.

*   *   *   *

A tear came into Cecil's eye and his chest heaved with pride as he played his brother's first (anonymous) recording. Jed and Gina couldn't help being moved either, as they held hands until the record finished enhancing the new understanding that had begun for them.

Cecil lifted the vinyl disc carefully and placed it back in a plain cover.

He was now ready to continue his story but not before they all enjoyed a dish of 'Jumbalaya' that he had prepared, 'to wash down the Bourbon!'

'There was no holding Louis,' he said, 'He was determined to record . . . .'

*   *   *   *

Cecil's story continued. Chicago 1927

There was no holding Louis. He was determined to record under his own name as well as playing his part in other bands. By now we were kind of indispensable so we went along as usual, Capone or no Capone, as he headed out to Chicago to meet up again with some of the old King Oliver band including the Dodds brothers, Johnny St Cyr and Lil Armstrong (nee Hardin and now married to Louis). Kid Ory (tb) replaced Dutrey on most sides but not all. According to the critics his place was taken by a certain 'John Thomas', well, there's a name for you! (He laughed)

Others say it may have been Gerald Reeves, brother of the fine trumpeter Reuben Reeves. (He paused for effect) But I know better. There may have been brothers involved but it wasn't them it was us. People who weren't there may well have got into a muddle over names I suppose, because Reuben was my brother's name as well. It was **May 1927**.

Louis just said, 'Do you think you can handle it Cecil?' I nearly took his arm off, I was so nervous I must admit. So that's how I took the Ory trombone role on those later Hot Five tracks such as 'Willie the Weeper'.

The band for 'Chicago Breakdown' at the same session was that of Carroll Dickerson, with a formidable line up including Louis and Bill Wilson (tpts) Dutrey & Cecil Solidar (tbs) Howard, Walker and Al Washington (saxes) (Reuben took Al's place because he was ill but I was a 'busking' addition) Hines, Basset, Hall and Briggs. As usual our contribution was not listed, but we were pleased to be paying our own small tribute to our New Orleans mentor, Ferdinand Lamott Morton 'Mr Jelly Roll' himself, who was the composer.

And that was my only entry into the 'Hall of Fame' and it's still disputed.

Here I've got a re-issue LP and we can listen to the whole session.

*　　*　　*　　*

Once more Jed and Gina sat patiently as 'Louis' weaved his magic and Cecil sat drinking Bourbon, and weeping in a chair. When it was over he looked at them as if he had finally proved a point that historians could not dispute. Jed was not so sure but he smiled approvingly as the precious disc was packed away. 'Now, where was I?' Cecil said.

*　　*　　*　　*

Cecil's story now in New York 1928-32

Oh yes, New York again. This time it was Joe 'King' Oliver himself who gave us a call. Louis was so busy here and there, that it seemed like a good opportunity to escape from the 'Windy City' once more. Oliver had an entirely new band all set to go for a residency and recordings in Harlem, but he was a bit concerned that his chosen sax and trombone might not materialise, so would we mind being the backup. What? Would we mind? We were off on the next train. The band was set to include Oliver and Nelson (tpts) Archey(tb) Holmes, Pacque & Jefferson (altos)

Frazier (tnr) Fry, Jones, Taylor and Walker. However, as it turned out he did get his full complement of stars, and we just kicked our heels until one day Charles Frazier was late for a recording session on 8 Oct 1929.

'We'd better send for the Ghost' said Joe, 'He can do the session until Charlie turns up. Studio time is money you know.' Ironically the first track to be recorded that day was 'Too Late', and it nearly was for Frasier because Reuben played a stormer. I could see Joe wondering whether he might make Reuben a permanent member of the band after that session. See, here on this record sleeve from RCA Camden (Oliver in Harlem), it lists the musicians and then says, 'Charles Frazier? Tenor sax.' Query, see? Once more they couldn't mention Reuben because of contracts but it did look as if he might get an offer to join the band full time, when tragedy struck and it was 'Too Late' after all, in more ways than one.

The first was this. It was less than a month later, on 29th October to be precise that New York changed from a bustling, busy community with plenty of work and smiles all around, to one of gloom, despair, unemployment and the return of a more vicious gangland culture. That day became known as 'Black Tuesday' as the bottom fell out of the Wall Street Stock market with a 12% drop in shares, and much more for some industries. Panic hid the streets as people tried to get their money out of the banks to no avail. This 'savings' panic didn't bother us, but it did when many of our musical haunts and bookings began to dry up.

The second problem was this. Oliver was in no hurry with an offer to Reuben now, probably because of contracts again, and he obviously would not want pay compensation in these more difficult times. So Reuben and me played around in the various 'dives' that remained open, as well as funerals, that showed no respect for the 'market'. It was barely enough to keep us ticking over so we took any job that came along.

It was then that we got to be aware that bookings were not the simple matter that they used to be. Just as Prohibition in Chicago in 1922 had ushered in a new gang warfare based on bootleg liquor so, now in 1929 in the 'Big Apple', some were quick to pick on adversity to make money, and they didn't mind how they did it either. We began to hear tales of organised crime, not just shadowy gangs slogging it out. Organised crime meant the 'Mafia' and the Mafia meant 'Lucky' Luciano. A pay off was usually called a 'percentage' and everyone paid if they wanted to live to an old age. There had been many rival 'organisations' in the protection racket but, one by one they accepted 'offers that they couldn't refuse' to join Luciano. This applied to booking agents just as it did to everyone else and refusal was a dangerous if not fatal business. Unfortunately one of our best agents, Zig Steiner did just that by agreeing to organise a lavish party on board the SS Steamboat 'Observation,' in the New York East River Basin for a Luciano rival named Mike 'Gloves' Modica who was an 'enforcer' for the 'Gambino' family. The Gambinos were thought to be expecting some 'favours' from the Republicans if they won the forthcoming election and likewise, the Genovese clan under Luciano were confident of 'special considerations' from the Democrats.

It was 1932 and coming up for election time when Reuben told me that he had 'business to attend to' and would be away for a week or so. He didn't say why, only that it was in Chicago so all I said was, 'Just make sure you're back for the 9th Sept or Paul won't be very pleased and nor shall I.' Well he did get back in time and his only comment was, 'It's good to get back to the uncomplicated world of music. You've no idea what a ruthless world it is out there.'

The band booked was 'Paul Lewis and his Society Syncopators, a band that Reuben and I were with at the time. It was a good outfit, a little bit smooth for us, but it could raise the roof for the 'Lindy Hop' which was the current rage following Charles Lindbergh's exploits. I'm telling you all this now because of what happened, but as far as we were concerned this was to be a welcome, and well paid 'Gig for Zig' on 9<u>th</u> Sept 1932.

Gina had been taking all this in of course and now she wanted to ask another question. 'Cecil.' she said, 'All of this politics, and gangsters and Mafia that Reuben was so preoccupied with. Did he suspect a connection, did others in the NAACP or similar groups also think as he did? Is that one of the reasons that the 'Highlander' group was formed in 1932, to confront racism? In other words was he a loner? I mean was he sticking his neck out further than others were prepared to do, or did he see or suspect something that most people didn't dream of? In other words is there a connection across legitimate and illegitimate society with a 'common cause,' namely the promotion of white supremacy not only in the USA but across nations. Is that just too fantastic or could it be true?'

(Here Cecil paused for a moment before replying. 'Let me go on' he said 'and then you can decide. Remember that these were difficult times.)

Author's note. *The Highlander Group was formed in 1932 in Tennessee as a 'folk school' to educate rural and industrial workers for a 'new social order'. It claimed to be a progressive labour movement in the South, including woodcutters, coal miners, textile workers and farmers but didn't fully integrate itself racially until 1942 when it cited that it's ethos was to 'confront racism and the evils of segregation.'*

When Cecil continued talking, it was as if he had been transported back to that very day on the river. He just closed his eyes and began to describe what took place in minute detail as if he was just an observer, and Jed and Melanie seemed to pass through a cloud to join him on the quayside of the East River Basin on that misty morning. He began 'Solly Steiner . . .

* * * *

'Solly' Steiner stood near the gangplank supervising loading of band gear when Reuben and Cecil turned up. Sol was 'Zig's' brother and they were a good team. Zig was the 'music man' and Sol took care of everything else including time schedules and the money.

'Good morning my friends,' he called out as they approached, 'I suppose you call this punctual. Trust you to be the last, we're nearly all loaded up and I was wondering if you'd decided to go off with that 'Armstrong' character again. We're not good enough for you these days are we?' Cecil looked at Reuben and said, 'Don't take any notice, he's always like this, a bit of a worrier you might say.' Then, turning to Sol he said, 'And a very good morning to you too, Solly. Now let's see, it's 9am now and, according to your very own timetable, the boat leaves at 10. What do you want us to do for an hour? Wash down the decks maybe?' Sol laughed and took them each by the arm. 'Of course not,' he said, 'It's so good to see you both, you know me, bark worse than bite. There's a hot chocolate in the Galley if you're chilled. Bar's not open yet I'm afraid.' Reuben smiled and patted his hip pocket, 'Don't worry Sol,' he said,' 'this isn't a Colt 45 in here you know. Just some provisions for the journey'

Saying this Reuben stepped on to the gangplank, staggering precariously to the deck above, closely followed by Cecil who seemed to be rather more stable even at this time of the morning. Of course, Reuben was not alone in 'taking a tipple' at breakfast, or any time for that matter. Reuben was one of those who claimed that alcohol was a necessary food, especially when preparing for a long band date. Cecil thought otherwise, preferring to keep all his faculties intact for the session. Anyway they made their way to the 'Band Deck' and sat down to 'set up' their instruments while engaging in chit-chat with some of the other band members who were already there. First to greet them was Paul Lewis, the bandleader who was already seated at the piano. 'Hi Guys,' he said, 'It's more of the usual today. Charts are on your stands except there's a new one that our hosts want us to play. It's called 'Ragusa Rag,' Why, you ask me, as if I should know? Why this Ziggy? Why that Ziggy? Well I do know as a matter of fact. Apparently Ragusa is a town in Sicily where part of the Modica family come from.' This was the first time that the brother's had heard the name of Zig's clients and it didn't mean anything to them at the time, but they were to find out a lot more later on.

Other musicians had also begun to set up their stands, often with little superstitious tokens, sometimes photos, sometimes trophies from a past gig (maybe a Garter), and sometimes even a 'prayer card.' Firstly the big beefy figure of Darnell Toms came over with a big grin. Not Louis perhaps, but a very strong trumpeter from New Orleans whom they had known for some time. 'Let's Shake it and Break it Fellas.' he said, 'I fancy a good hot session today, how about you?' They agreed with lots of backslapping until little Moshie Green spoke up. He was the archetypal symphonic violinist and naturally a brilliant musician. 'Just don't forget the dots this time Cecil.' he said rather ruefully because he knew that Cecil was short sighted and had been excused 'The Draft' because of it.

They were all soon assembled in neat rows and in smart band uniforms looking a bit like a Regiment from the 12th Hussars, white jackets with red horizontal stripes, white trousers and black shoes. Red socks added a distinctive if less military flavour. There were two trumpets, a trombone, two saxophones/clarinets, two violins, piano, bass, banjo and drums and then there was Ruby Starr, the 'glamorous vocaliste'.

Could she sing? Well, did it matter? Now the band was finally ready, the guests were on board and Paul started up with 'On the Sunnyside of the Street' despite the gloom and the drizzle. Fortunately the Deck area was mostly covered over, so the guests could move around in relative comfort. Later on they would go down to the dining area, and the band would join them to play some relaxing 'dinner music' with 'Ruby's Romantic Renditions.'

It was a very 'dressy' affair with most men in dress suits and women in long gowns, some neat and starched and some on the voluptuous side. It just didn't do to ask who was with whom at a do like this.

The day had brightened up considerably by midday as the vessel hove to before turning back to port, so people were able to sit out in the sun while the band took a break. Everyone seemed in convivial mood and a large amount of alcohol was consumed, and not just by the band. Cecil was a bit worried about Reuben. He was about 5 minutes older, they had been told, and funnily enough it was indeed Cecil who was the more responsible, whilst his younger sibling played his part by 'fooling around.' It was Cecil who always got them out of trouble if he hadn't managed to avoid it in the first place. Once more he thought that he should speak up. 'Don't you think you've had enough?' he asked calmly.

'Don't worry,' came the reply, 'look, I can stand can't I?' and Reuben got to his feet, swaying a little more than the boat in the swell of the river.

'Just watch it,' said his brother, 'We're on in a minute, I hope you can play your instrument.' Perhaps Cecil should have known better because Reuben was a master, drunk or sober, and so it was when they struck up with 'Ain't she Sweet' and Reuben took a very tasteful muted trumpet solo before the vocal. 'That's my boy.' thought Cecil.

So the Steamship began it's journey back and the guests gathered below decks for a sit-down meal around a single long table covered with a white tablecloth in the middle of the room. The band was ready to play again and this is where they had been asked to play the Sicilian song that had been requested. Paul got to his feet and waved his baton confidently, 'One, Two, Three.' he began but got no further as a hail of machine gun bullets strafed the top table. There was general panic and this time the band did stop playing and took cover. It had suddenly gone very dark, and there was a smell of acrid smoke that penetrated the room, making it very difficult to breathe. Then, as if it had just been waiting for the end of an overture, the whole room burst into flames. Cecil looked around for Reuben but he could not see him. Meanwhile Reuben was desperately trying to find Cecil but again it was to no avail, the whole ship was burning. It was only about 50 yards offshore but the port fire crews could not reach the stricken vessel because of the heat. Some passengers and crew managed to jump clear but many more were trapped as the steamer sank partially in the dock. This extinguished some of the flames and at last the rescue services could come on board. It was not a pretty sight but there was worse to come. After about half an hour of burning and bubbling, the vessel seemed to give a big heave and suddenly exploded in a shower of sparks and smoke that could be seen for miles.

(Authors note. *The Steamboat 'SS Observation' exploded in the New York East River on September 9th 1932. 71 persons were killed*)

None of the guests survived but a few members of the crew and some musicians made it to the shore including Moshie Green, Darnell Toms, Daniel Figueraro, Giusseppe Zangara, Ruby Starr and the Solidar brothers. The bodies of Ziggy and Solly Steiner were found in the hold unmarked by fire, but with their throats cut and a musical manuscript in each mouth. Nearby were two more bodies with the letters 'ALL' cut into their faces. The body of Paul Lewis was never recovered. The wounded including Reuben, were taken immediately to Hospital and it was feared for a time that he would not recover from his severe burns. Cecil maintained a constant vigil, willing his brother to get well. Gradually he did, his breathing improved and soon his bandages would be removed. On that day the doctor called Cecil to one side. 'We've done all we can for him.' he said 'He's lucky to be alive you know but we can't do anything about his face. Try not to look shocked. He's going to be like that for the rest of his life, so try not to make it worse for him. Fortunately, his mouth and lips are not badly damaged so he should still be able to play if he wants to. He may need your encouragement for that. Let's go in shall we?' Eventually and after many months, Reuben did recover and he did play again, though not in public, as we shall find out.

Naturally there was a massive investigation, which eventually concluded that it was a gangland assassination attempt that had not turned out as expected. The Steiner murders were deemed to be 'territorial' warnings. The 'ALL' disfigurements were not explained, but taken to be a final warning from some crazy gangster. No one was ever apprehended or tried for these crimes. With the death of the 'Modica' faction, the 'Gambino' clan was fatally weakened, and Luciano's control had become virtually unassailable. But was this enough to secure a Democratic win as well?

* * * *

After this 'virtual diversion' Cecil was ready to continue his story but Gina could see that he was tired and, she thought, apt to get a bit muddled so, turning to Jed she said, 'That's such a lot to take in Jed and I'm rather tired. Do you think we might continue the story in a few days?' Cecil looked a bit disappointed as if, now that he had got someone to listen, he did not want to let them go but Jed spoke up to support Gina.

'I think that's a good idea Cecil. We need to go through some of these tape recordings so that we've got the story straight. Would it be all right if we came back after about a week. I'd rather like to check up on some of the missing bits in your story that might help.' Finally Cecil agreed and, thanking him, they set a date to continue in a week's time.

Jed and Gina decide to investigate the fire.

When they got home they slumped onto the large comfy settee together and both said 'Phew!' at the same time. It had been a roller coaster and it wasn't even half way through Cecil's story yet. Gina spoke first, 'Do you know what I'd like now?' she asked. Jed smiled and responded by nuzzling her neck. 'I think so Darling but why don't I run a nice hot bath first? You get in and I'll join you with some 'Champers'' 'You do say the nicest things,' she said, 'but let's have a little cuddle here first.' Jed was about to agree when he realised that she was fast asleep.

At breakfast Gina said that she would type out a duplicate copy of Cecil's story to date so that they could both study it at the same time.

Jed meanwhile planned to visit the Library to look at some of the items in the Newspapers that might have a bearing. He decided to start in 1932 in New York to see what was said about the fire on the Riverboat. The information in the Central library was contained on microfiche spools so it took a little time for Jed to find his way. This turned out to be fortunate because, as he searched for 1932 in the New York Times, his gaze settled on 1933 instead, and a name 'leapt out' at him from the pages there.

It was 'Giusseppe Zangara' who, according to the report had made an assassination attempt on the Republican President Roosevelt. He had missed but killed the Mayor of Chicago. Prior to becoming President FDR had been Mayor of New York so the paper felt doubly affronted. Jed's mind was buzzing. Now where had he seen that name before? Where? Where, damn it? He made a note to check Cecil's story when he got home and now moved swiftly back to 1932. As Cecil had said there had been two mysterious deaths with their faces marked with the letters 'ALL'. The paper didn't expand further on this, again as Cecil had told them, but it did give the names of the dead men. They were Frank Dewey and Alvin Stoller, both said to be of Chicago. Again Jed was puzzled. Why were Chicago mobsters on a New York steamboat? Could be any reason he supposed but what if there was another link? As for the 'ALL' mutilations, Jed already knew through his work that this group had not declared itself publicly as 'The All American League' until 1934, taking on the mantle of the waning KKK. Prior to that it was suspected of acting as an 'action mob' for a number of other organizations including the Mafia, providing 'soldiers' when called upon. But why were Dewey and Stoller the victims here? And where did 'Zangara' fit in?

(Authors note. *Zangara shot and killed Anton Cermak the Mayor of Chicago on 15th Feb 1933.*)

Jed decided to call off his library search for now and head home. He still couldn't place Zangara and he hoped that Gina's transcript would solve that particular mystery. She was still at her work when he arrived home but they soon found the name. Giuseppe Zangara had been one of the members of the Paul Lewis Band on board the SS 'Observation' on that terrible night of the fire, and was one of the few to escape. If he had been involved with the fire or any of the killings it seemed more than likely that he was a 'Luciano' Mafia agent attempting to derail the FDR Presidency, and having failed on the boat, he tried again a year later.

Perhaps he was also the killer of Dewey and Stoller in his role for the 'ALL'. But there again, why draw attention to these particular killings? It was a puzzle all right. Who was being warned? Who did Zangara know well enough to want to give a warning to rather than a shot to the head?

Jed was puzzled and it was Gina who made the first suggestion.

'I reckon it was a warning to Reuben,' she said, 'members of the band probably all knew of his membership of the NAACP and the support that they had given to Lafollette in the 1924 Election and didn't Cecil say that Reuben went to Chicago just before this one. Here, look at this 1932 Almanac. It shows that there were two left wing parties standing, the Socialists and the Communists and, if the 'Luciano' aim was to help the Democrats, it would be helpful to remove one or both of these groups as they would be likely to take some of the Democrat, not Republican vote. So anyone who supported them, such as the NAACP should be stopped, but in Reuben's case, just warned. Being band members they might have been quite close friends. I wonder if he was the other saxophonist?'

Jed gave her a puzzled look, but it was also rather an admiring one.

'Well, you've certainly got a conspiracy theory there,' he said, 'Now if we knew that Dewey and Stiller were NAACP agents you might prove your point.' That was like a red rag to a bull but she responded in a quiet and dignified way, 'Patience Jedsy Lomax,' she said, 'just you wait and see and then you can apologise.'

'I certainly will,' he replied, 'but actually there's another organisation and leader that could be involved, and that's the 'National Union of Social Justice' headed by that zealous Roman Catholic priest, Father Coughlin. His radio sermons had been praising Hitler and Mussolini for some time and his newspaper 'Social Justice' sold more than a million copies broadcasting mainly anti-Semitic propaganda. His was a voice of hate closely linked to the German American Bund. By 1939 he was leading an armed militia known as the 'Christian Front' (a la Falange in Spain). Maybe it's stretching it a bit to link all these disparate groups together but one thing's for sure. If they ever did get together it would be disastrous.'

Unknown to Jed at that time he had hit on the truth. They had got together. They were together and had been so, undetected for more than a century. The reality was so unbelievable that it wasn't even considered by those who might have made a difference. At that time there was a great deal of 'isolationism' in America and in Europe, and many of the States within the USA were barely on speaking terms in matters of racial policy.

Jed decided that there wasn't much more they could do then and there, so at last he decided to call it a day and began to run a bath, 'Are you awake this time my darling?' he called from the steam clouds in the bathroom. 'I certainly am my sweet.' she replied, 'can't you see?' Well he couldn't actually as his glasses had steamed up as well, so he just reached out towards the door searching blindly for the handle. But it wasn't the door that his outstretched fingers came into contact with, but a warm pliant body in that robe that fell to the floor again as his fingers touched her.

Cecil's story contd. 1933-41.

A couple of days later they were back at Cecil's apartment and he couldn't wait to carry on where he had left off. Once more they sat in silence as he told them about the aftermath of the Riverboat fire.

'There's no easy way to say this' he began . . . .

There's no easy way to say this because I loved my brother, but he was a grotesque sight after the fire, like Quasimodo without the hump. People shivered when they saw him. Even close friends couldn't bear to be near him. Of course that affected his confidence, so, for many months I practised with him, just the two of us in private. Strangely I think he began to play better and better as if to compensate for his affliction so I was very pleased when we got another call from Fletcher Henderson, then in Chicago for a recording session. I didn't like to remind him that it had been ten years since that session in New York, but I did ask him if he knew about Reuben's accident and disfigurement. 'Yes I do know,' he said, 'but who sees faces on recordings? This job is a very special one ideally suited to Reuben's particular skill and phrasing. Mind you the part is for clarinet but I don't expect any problems there. I'm looking for a new sound you see and there's an unofficial part for you in the trombones if you like.' I was over the moon, for myself yes but especially for Reuben. The track to be recorded was 'Wrappin it Up' and it was a great musical, though not commercial success. That success would come soon after, with the same sound but with a totally different band in New York many years later.

I'll just digress here for a moment to complete the 'Moonlight' story. It's been said that nearly all music is plagiaristic to a certain degree but there can't be many more blatant copies than the arrangement for 'Moonlight Serenade' by the Glenn Miller band. Glenn had seemingly listened to and liked Fletcher's 'Wrappin' it up' and he obviously knew that it was Reuben who provided that sweet clarinet sound. What better way could there be to emulate it than to ask Reuben to join him for his recording in 1939. It meant going to New York again but the money was good, very good and Glenn knew that Reuben would only do the recording. Of course the melody was totally different, but the arrangement in which the clarinet took the normal trumpet lead, thereby giving a softer sound, was what Glenn was after.

(Authors note. *Some people said that this part was played by Wilbur Schwartz*)

I'll tell you later how we came to join the Miller band during the War years, but it was 'my' Reuben who made that first recording with Glenn in 1939 and Pee Wee Erwin's trumpet was reduced to 'second fiddle'. (Cecil laughed at his own joke).

Well anyway after the Henderson success, it was me who got a big break. Remember Reuben wasn't playing in public so I was doing a lot of session work and I was very pleased to receive a call from Roy Fox, him of the 'Whispering Trumpet' and the 'Darling' of LA. He had taken a band to London in 1930 and now wanted some replacements over there. His band included Jack Jackson and Lew Davis (a favourite of mine) as well as the 'heart throb' of the decade, Al Bowlly. Venues included all the top spots in London such as the Café de Paris in Coventry Street, the 'Monseigneur' off Piccadilly Circus, the 'Carlton' and the 'Café Anglais' where we played to the elites of British Society including the Prince of Wales. Reuben was with me naturally but, as he still couldn't play in public, he used to frequent the many low jazz dives in the City at night and here he picked up rumour and gossip, gossip and rumour, much of it about Prince and his 'lady friend' Mrs Wallis Simpson, as well as the latest on the street about the rise of Fascism in Europe. 'It's not only in the States that the Black Man is a second class citizen' he told me. 'Over here it's the Jews as well.' I told you that Reuben was likely to get himself into trouble but I was too busy with one important Dance or Ball after another to take much notice. We were especially busy in the month of May 1933 with the 'London Conference' attended by many world leaders including Ciano from Italy and some minor royals such as some relations of the Rainiers from Monaco, and those ousted Romanovs who couldn't say no to a party These characters seemed to get on very well, I'd say they might easily have been conspirators, the way they huddled up and passed notes to and fro. Later we went on to the 'Silver Jubilee State Ball' at Buckingham Palace and there I saw for myself that the Duke was sailing close to the wind with his affair when I noticed the old King (George V) frowning conspicuously as the couple waltzed by. When I told

Reuben he just said, 'I'm not surprised. It's not just the King but the Government too, and not just about the affair either. It seems that the Duke holds 'court' at many 'political receptions' in the houses of friends such as the Londonderry's in Park Lane, and not only that, but that his 'hideaway home' at 'The Fort' in Windsor Great Park is another meeting place, not just of friends but, let's say, of 'like minded' individuals. Another strange matter is that Mr Ernest Simpson is often at the 'Fort' when the Duke is 'entertaining' his wife. Rumour has it that they share other common interests on the International stage, Simpson being a major American shipping magnate with eyes and ears in every port across the Globe.' I suppose I thought nothing of it and that Reuben tended to see conspiracies anywhere and everywhere and, as I said, usually the next gig was just around the corner and so it was, Paris.

(Authors note. *Some details from Wallis Simpson's Diaries*)

Out of the blue (he continued) we both got an offer to play with the Teddy Hill Band in Paris and, as we were already in London, it appealed to Reuben because we'd heard that Paris was a place where black jazz musicians were especially welcome, albeit in part as members of the somewhat vaudevillian 'Blackbirds' show. We were over the moon when Reuben was asked to take part in a recording under the name of the superb trombonist Dicky Wells, to be called 'Dicky Wells in Paris.' Also there was Bill Coleman but more especially for us, the idiosyncratic 'gypsy' guitarist Django Reinhardt. Reuben shared three tracks with the alto of Howard Johnson a week later with Roger Chaput on Guitar. I don't know why the personnel changed. (It was July 1937).

We stayed in Europe for a while and were lucky enough to join the British bandleader Jack Hylton Band on his tour in 1938 that included a concert appearance at 'The Scala Theatre' in Berlin. He had just completed a series of radio broadcasts for the American market and had been obliged to use American musicians due to work permit restrictions, and that's how he came to know us. However, he took a mixed band to Germany including Billy Ternent and another fine vocalist, Sam Browne. The rows were full of uniformed officers of the SA and the SS and their ladies and we both found the atmosphere rather threatening. It was rumoured that 'Il Duce' was to be guest of honour then, that it would be the Duke of Windsor (then in Salzburg), and lastly 'Der Fuehrer' himself, but actually it turned out to be Joseph Goebbells, the Minister of Propoganda. With him was Leni Riefenstahl, the architect of the Nuremburg Rallies with their theme 'The Triumph of the Will.' In fact the theatre was bedecked in much the same way with rectangular flags with Nazi emblems covering the walls. For those who haven't seen such a flag up close, I can tell you it's a scary sight. It's a white flag with a singular red circle in the centre and in the circle is a black swastika. We couldn't wait to get out of there.

We knew little of European affairs of course but you've probably gathered by now that Reuben was not one to let unfairness and inhumanity rest. So when he heard about and even witnessed pro Nazi and anti Semitic groups, his blood boiled over and he was soon in trouble with the authorities. To cut a long story short we were soon classed as 'undesirables' and on our way home.

I was rather glad about that because young Reuben, my son had just started at the Julliard School of Music. It was a far cry from the way we started out, but I wanted to give him the best chance that I could. He seemed a natural, just like his uncle and I felt proud of him also.

As I said, Reuben began to be in demand but the next call was another surprise, from Jimmy Lunceford back in the States, to take the place of Joe Thomas who was sick. The record was' Harlem Shout' and it's a knockout, just great for the 'jitterbug (here Cecil attempted to demonstrate but nearly fell over). Up and up, next it was 'The Highness of Hi de Ho' none other than Cab Calloway himself. Cab's band bordered on the manic borderlines of comedy including his own vocal on 'Minnie the Moocher' that was a great success. However, in that band he had one of the very best tenor sax players at that time, namely Chu Berry. After Coleman Hawkins and Lester Young he had few equals and it was Cab Calloway who wanted to showcase his star performer in a ballad somewhat reminiscent of Coleman Hawkins' 'Body and Soul,' which was widely recognised as a masterpiece.

The tune chosen was 'Ghost of a Chance'. This was not an easy piece at all, for example there is a key change in the middle eight and there was some initial doubt that Chu wanted to record it, preferring 'Stardust' or some other, but Cab was insistent. 'We need something that will define you as a soloist,' he said, 'not another version of just another song.' The story goes that Chu would only agree if Cab sent for 'The Ghost' to help with the complicated chord changes prior to the recording. Reuben told me that Cab asked them to do a 'take' each in turn, and then again and again and again. Each time he said, 'Yes that's better, Yes, that's better.' until he seemed satisfied and asked Reuben to do a last 'take' with the whole band, and when he'd finished, he turned to Chu and just said, 'Now Leon, let's see what you've got in your locker.'

The band struck up and Berry delivered a masterpiece. I have it here but before I play it, let me tell you what Cab told me in confidence.

('I can tell you Cecil (he said) that it was a privilege to hear them trading ideas until the final recordings. They left together and went off to have a drink somewhere I suppose. Anyway I turned to the recording engineer and told him to prepare a master disc for Chu's performance. I was staggered at his reply. 'Which one was it?' he asked. 'Didn't you number them?' I retorted angrily. 'No,' he said, 'You didn't ask me to.' So there I was with two versions in front of me. I asked him to play them through and through, but when I thought I'd got it, I heard something that changed my mind. I sat there for hours. Everyone except the engineer had gone home and he was getting rather annoyed. Finally I made my choice, ticked the box and handed one version over. 'It's that one,' I said, 'I'm sure of it. Master that one.' He muttered something like, thank goodness for that, and went back to the recording area. Eventually it was released to great acclaim, but I'm telling you this, sworn to secrecy of course, that I was not sure at all, and it could well be Reuben (The Ghost) Solidar's 'Ghost of a Chance' that was a hit, not Chu Berry's. That would have been very appropriate don't you think?')

Cecil paused, picked up the disc and said, 'See what you think.' When it finished they could see that he was quite certain that it was Reuben and he said as much. 'There, you can tell it's him can't you?' and they just had to agree. Satisfied, Cecil moved on to his next extraordinary tale.

A little while back I told you about the 'Miller Moonlight Serenade' with Reuben on clarinet. It's just one of those sounds that just caught on and Glenn told Reuben there was a place for him in the band on a permanent basis if only he could get some treatment. Of course this was out of the question but funny things happen sometimes, because soon after the recording Reuben got a very unexpected call from Duke Ellington.

Now let me tell you about Reuben and 'The Duke'. Everyone knows that Ellington only employed the very best, and Ben Webster (tenor sax) had been added sometime between October 1939 and February 1940, so it was a big surprise for Reuben to get a call. Apparently the Duke wanted to give a party for Billy Strayhorn, his musical partner and there was only a piano in the flat. 'We want to try out a few new things,' the Duke said, 'Ben's away and it's that sound that we're looking for. Will you do it?' Of course Reuben agreed, and this is what he told me afterwards.

'The party had gone fine and it was getting late . . . .

*   *   *   *

The Party had gone fine and it was getting late when the Duke strolled over to the piano and started to play the 'Blues.' The noise and chatter subsided a bit and then Billy walked across and sat beside the 'master.'

The talking seemed to stop and a small crowd gathered around as Billy set up a counter melody to the Duke, who responded with an outrageous harmonic twist that made me smile. 'Ladeez and Geentlemen,' said the Duke from his sedentary position, 'Tonight we have Mr Reuben Solidar on tenor sax sitting in for Ben. I think that you all know about the fire accident some years back, but here he is playing better than ever.' That was some introduction coming from the Duke so I began to play, a little hesitantly at first, and then with more confidence as my two accompanists set up a kind of Creole rhythm behind me. Then, just as I was finding my way, I realised that they were extending the normal 12 bar blues by an extra bar each chorus. 'Cheeky monkeys' I thought, 'Trying to catch me out are you?' I soon picked up the idea but no sooner had I done so, than it changed again, 4 bars off, then 3 bars on. They were having a whale of a time, then my ears pricked up a different modulation and I had only seconds to recognize it. Yes it was their composition 'Solitude.' I greeted it with a big mournful tenor sound and I could see them smiling as if to say 'Yes, this Reuben knows his stuff and some.' When it was over the Duke said, 'I think someone recorded that. Hey Frankie, did you get that?' Frank nodded his head and the Duke looked pleased. 'Of course if it ever comes out it'll be Ben on the label. Hope you don't mind?' Of course I said I didn't, but then he added something that made my hair stand on end. 'I can't give you a contract.' he said, 'but I can do something for you and I'm going to.' Remember this was Edward 'Duke' Ellington, the foremost bandleader in the land. What could he do for me?

'I have a friend.' he said, 'Dr Abel Livsey, top jazz fan but also one of the most eminent plastic surgeons in the land. Now. No arguments. You're booked in next week at his clinic here and it's all paid for, on me. Cecil has taken care of all of your band jobs for the next three months and you should be on the road in no time.' I just didn't know what to say. It seemed that everything had been taken care of and you, my big brother were part of it. What can I say but 'Thanks a million' to you, and to the Duke. Here, let me play the Louis version for you.' And he did.

Cecil took up the story again but didn't have much to add, except to say that Reuben had undergone his treatment with no complaints and had found a quartet job off the Bronx where he was soon drawing a crowd. Also that he wasn't sure if the treatment was a Miller-Ellington' gift. However he had now become quite tearful and tried to explain how much he loved his brother and how the music that they shared had brought them so close. And yet, he went on to explain, there was another driving *force* in Reuben's life that Cecil did not share and this had kept them apart in some sense. So where was love if we didn't share trust, he mused? There was no getting away from it, he was convinced that he had failed his brother on this, the most important thing in life, and must now try to make amends. He took a deep breath before he continued.

'Yes I did know that he'd been involved in politics and race related issue but he didn't talk much about it. So, when he said he was going to see KoKo (Billy Shu) in LA I didn't put two and two together. I suppose I thought it was a gig of some sort and now he's dead and I blame myself. I didn't support him you see, I rather hoped all these troubles would go away, so he carried quite a burden. If you love someone you should support that person shouldn't you? I don't mean agree necessarily, but I should have been there for him shouldn't I? Way back, when he told me about the NAACP, I walked away and he never confided in me again. Of course I realise now that he was only trying to protect me, as maybe he got more involved and closer to those shadowy figures at the top. So you see why I must find out what happened. You will help won't you?'

Gina held his hand between hers and said, 'Yes we will. We said we would and we will. We've arranged to see Billy in LA tomorrow so no more worries now. We'll be back soon to let you know what we find out.'

Jed and Gina go to LA

Jed and Gina arrived at the LA main rail terminal still unsure as to how to proceed. They had discussed the case on the train but they were not that much wiser. What did Cecil really expect them to find out? At least they had a starting point, and that was Kojiro (KoKo) Shu the 'Billy' Shu that Cecil had mentioned. He lived at 2222 Columbia and Akiro, KoKo's wife met them with a broad smile and traditional greeting.

'Konnichiwa (hello) Lomax San and welcome to our most humble home.' she said. 'Hello Akiro,' replied Jedsy, 'It is so good to meet you. This is my friend Gina.' 'And this is my husband Kojiro.' said Akiro, 'Let's all go in and have tea, please to follow me.' They followed her into what, by western standards, you would call a sparsely furnished room but in Japan it would have been the norm. A large round table was in the centre of the room but it was only two foot high, meaning that all persons seated at said table sat on the floor and not on chairs. Akiro motioned them to sit while she left the room. The Shu's were very cosmopolitan, modern Japanese it's true, but it was still Akiro who went out to make the tea; with rice cakes. Kojiro spoke first. 'Firstly I would like to say how pleased we are that you have come to help us and to find Reuben's killer of course. Arigato, thank you.' Well this wasn't at all what Jed expected. As far as he knew, Cecil had merely asked him to find out if there was anything unusual about Reuben's death and now the plot had thickened. 'Of course we'll do what we can.' said Gina, speaking for them both as Akiro returned, now in a beautiful white kimono with dragons, carrying a large tray with cups and a teapot. 'I hope you don't mind, honoured guests,' she began, 'but we would like to show you ancient Japanese ritual. Our heritage is important to us although we should be called American-Japanese, not Japanese-American as everyone says these days. It seems to be a way of vilifying us in words as well as in actions. Every day KoKo go to work at Ford dealership, children sing Stars and Stripes at school and I'm a teacher there. We are Americans but the war has denied us even this.'

She knelt down and then nestled backwards on her legs from which position she could still lean forward to serve the tea. Jed & Gina were cross-legged as was KoKo, and it was surprisingly comfortable. KoKo now spoke up with a few introductory words about the ceremony.

'Now don't feel nervous about protocol, just follow Akiro's example and you'll soon get the idea. Tradition is very big in Japan and especially so with Japanese families who have made their home abroad. I suppose it keeps us in touch with our roots. Because there's only four of us this particular ceremony would be called a 'chakai'. There are different words for larger groups, some of which even include Saki, but sorry, none today.' He laughed as he saw Jed looking around for the very small cups in which the rice drink would have been served. 'Sorry, Lomax San, maybe later.' Now they all laughed as KoKo continued. 'Each ceremony actually means 'The way of the tea.' It's always green tea, or 'sado' in Japanese. The small water bowls are for you to purify your hands and, of course we all took our shoes off when coming in. So we can start.'

The ceremony took place in some seriousness and relative silence, and in some ways it helped Jed&Gina to settle in and to feel comfortable. It seemed like Akiro and Kojiro had gone into a trance as they closed their eyes with just the occasional movement to suggest that they were not asleep. After what seemed like quite a long time, Akiro got to her feet and motioned them to follow her a few paces to where cushions were laid on the floor and on which everyone now sat. Soon the conversation turned to Reuben's visit and the situation in LA after Pearl Harbour. According to KoKo there was an immediate outpouring of hostility to them and their neighbours, many of which were third or even fourth generation citizens. The Government actually used this as an excuse for internment, 'for your own protection' they said, but that's not how it seemed to him.

'Just imagine Jedsy San.' he said. 'What would you and your family feel like if the Government locked up Gina and her family, which they still might do I suppose since the US is at war with them as well. At the moment, as far as I know, German and Italian Americans have to register and carry ID cards, and also be prepared to move if they live in California near any docks or military bases. There seems to be 'special treatment' for us because of the raid on US soil I suppose. Just ask Akiro.'

'Yes' she said,' Sofu and Sobo were given just two days to leave their home where they had lived for thirty years, and they were only allowed to take bare essentials. They are now in the Tule Lake camp. Just imagine it, Sobu is over sixty and I don't think that she'll survive this.' She was very upset and had started to cry so Gina moved to comfort her as KoKo picked up the story, 'She means Grandpa and Grandma.' he explained, 'There are now more than 100,000 in the camps where they have been sent for 'screening'. It's such an outrage, that many groups such as the NAACP are volunteering to help us, and that's what Reuben did. Akiro and me are still here because he pulled some strings because she is 8 months pregnant, as you can see.' He smiled lovingly and proudly at his wife and continued.' After the baby I suppose we'll have to go but God knows where.'

'Let me see if I've got this right.' Jed said. 'More than 100,000 have been removed from California to camps for screening. What about afterwards? Are they still there?' KoKo replied with a shrug. 'Who knows?' he said. 'There is talk of resettlement in the mid west but when we do not know, and how could Sobu and Sofu manage a farm?'

All this seemed too much for Gina who now had become quite animated.

'I'm not surprised that there were disturbances.' she said, 'Not at all, but the Press in New York have kept the lid on it I can tell you.' KoKo shrugged his shoulders. 'Actually there wasn't much to start with. I think that we were all too shocked. That's why the NAACP and other groups were so helpful in getting us organised. You see, the Government did recognise two groups within our community, but having done that they treated them more or less the same. We are 'Nesei' the group born here. The other group were classified 'Issei' and not eligible for naturalisation, in other words, economic migrants to the US.'

Jed felt it was time to move on to Reuben's role in the situation and he was especially keen to find out some background, as well as what actually happened on the day that he was found dead. Akiro paused for a moment before she agreed. 'I'd like to tell you what happened if KoKo agrees. (he nodded) We must not leave anything out so I want you to imagine the scene as Reuben arrived on Valentines Day. Be patient and let me tell you in my own words. 'It was a lovely bright, wintry day . . . .

Akiro's story Los Angeles.

t was a lovely bright wintry day on February 14th 1942 when Reuben arrived at the flat greeted at the door by Kojiro. 'Come in and most welcome Reuben San' she said. They knew each other quite well because of the many band jobs that he and Kojiro (KoKo) had done together, and they planned to do a special musical get together that evening at a local bar for a Valentines Day supper. Naturally everyone dresses up as 'Gangster or Moll' for such occasions but few would have experienced it in reality as Reuben and KoKo had. They were looking forward to that but first of all they had business to discuss about the internments and how Reuben might be able to help. You might wonder how it was that the NAACP (National Association Advancement Coloured Peoples) came to be involved but it wasn't so strange really. From their foundation in 1909 their concern was with all 'Coloured' in other words, non white persons in the US. Amongst their founders were many Civic leaders of Jewish, Latino or Native American backgrounds, not just Afro-American.

Kojiro explained to Reuben that there were many ordinary folk who were glad to 'beat up on' individuals in their community because the Pearl Harbour raid had been presented by the President as an 'Act of Infamy' rather than an act of war because of the delay in a formal declaration of hostilities. KoKo thought that if this had not been the case the JA, (Japanese Americans) might have been treated in the same way as other belligerent nations such as Germany or Italy. He added that, where there is such unease amongst normal law abiding folk, it doesn't take much to make matters worse by groups inciting violence. On this occasion the crowds that filled the streets with rowdy youths, broken bottles and some Molotov cocktails were unrecognisable as an organised force. They seemed to be just 'Patriotic Americans' and that's about the only slogan you could see except 'Japs Out' or 'Nips Die'. Shops were looted but the Press seemed to under some pressure not to report the worst atrocities.

The first thing that Reuben said he could do to help was to explain to Kojiro that these were not disorganised groups at all but probably undercover KKK (Ku Klax Klan) or maybe ALL (American Liberation League) agents sent to foment discord. There had also been hints of an even larger international organisation involved. These groups had used these tactics since the 1920's, waxing and waning over the years. Here they had seen a new chance to re-establish white supremacy in California and of course, elsewhere. Reuben added that the NAACP had more recently become aware of a more sinister co-ordinating force alleged to have political and economic clout, as well as a wider international dimension. 'The best thing that we can do is to play them at their own game.' he said, 'I'll set up some organizing committees and we'll bring a few 'heavies; down to help out.' Now KoKo looked alarmed, 'Oh please no, nothing like that. No violence please. Haven't we had enough trouble already?' Reuben looked at KoKo and then at me, 'Don't worry,' he said, 'It's only for self defence.'

The next few days and weeks were a cat and mouse game between the two sides, each trying to outsmart the other whist staying within the law. It seemed to some and certainly to Reuben, as he told us, that law enforcement was hardly colour-blind here. Many of the JA protestors and NAACP helpers were arrested but hardly any of the opposition gangs. However the battle was not being fought on the streets alone. Reuben and a small committee had managed to infiltrate the command structure of 'ALL' in their HQ at San Bernadino just outside LA and this was the report of their 'mole'.

'Report of meeting held at Pasadena Hotel on April 1st 1942 (April Fools Day) in the name of 'The Pearl Harbour Patriots.' By Zeb Clowsky.

Meeting started at 8pm but bar had been well used before then. Probably more than 100 persons and all vetted thoroughly at the door, including me. No badges or insignias of flags or bunting and seemingly a rather modest home spun kind of gathering at first. I did talk to some delegates and they had come from far and wide to hear the main speaker. I did not like to ask too many questions but it soon became apparent that the speaker was to be 'The Chief' and this seemed to carry enormous weight in the room. 'First time I've seen him,' said one. 'First public appearance this year.' someone else said. I did venture a small suggestion about his identity, as no one else seemed likely to do so. 'I've heard he's the boss of 'ALL' and MD of Anglo American Oil.' I said, somewhat on a fishing expedition, and then wished I hadn't.

The group I was with looked at me suspiciously and laughed out loud.

'See these?' said one, showing me his knuckles. It was a bit gloomy so I took it to be a threat especially as the other three in the group did the same. But no, I could then see in the gloom, that all of them had the three letters ALL on their knuckles and were proud to show me. 'Think we don't know our own leaders?' said another one, and then a third, 'Well we do and the 'The Chief' isn't one of them.' the fourth man added, 'We don't know who he is, we don't need to know and he wants it to stay that way. It's not good business to ask questions so be careful. By the way, who are you?' I made my cover identity known and it seemed to satisfy them, but I realised it was a close run thing. Shortly afterwards the speeches began, usual KKK 'crap' and then it was time to meet 'The Chief.' Strangely enough the introductory music was 'Land of Hope and Glory,' harking back, I suppose to a British 'racist' Empire that ruled half the world. What were they up to, these men in the shadows I thought?

I said that it was 'a bit gloomy' earlier but, as two figures mounted the platform, the lights dimmed even more, so much so that no features could be identified at all. I tried to get closer but a few frowns warned me off again. Then 'The Chief' stood and the room went so quiet you could hear a feather drop. As I said, he was in the shade but I would say that he was over six foot tall and rather angular in his frame, a bit like Abraham Lincoln in stature but nothing like him in what he had to say. He began, 'This land is ours. This land is not theirs. Now repeat after me, 'This land is ours.' The crowd responded. 'Now repeat after me again. This land is not theirs. Repeat!' The crowd loved it and did as they were bid. He raised his hand 'Duce' fashion. 'My friends' he said, 'Our mission is simple, it is a temporal but also a spiritual journey in which, God willing, we will be re-united with our soil as one.' It sounded like a passage from Mein Kampf to me but there was more, and each time he stopped the crowd bayed out, 'This land is ours. This land is not theirs.' He raised his hand again and spoke. 'My friends, my colleagues, my agents, for that is what you are. You are the agents through which our goal will be accomplished, but not only here. It has begun in Europe but may not succeed there for the present without some intervention from us in the highest places, but I'll say no more about that now. They call me the Chief <u>but I am not worthy</u> to stand in the shoes of he who is behind me, he who existed before me and will exist after me 'Our Glorious

Leader' whom you will all get to know in due course.' (Here Clowsky added a note. '*See Biblical reference John the Baptist and Jesus*'.)

The Chief continued, 'Just as you look at the sullen black man and the Jew with their crafty faces, now look on the treacherous slit eyes of the Oriental and hate! Yes, say after me. Hate. Hate. Hate!' Once more the crowd obeyed and waved arms at the dark platform. I looked around to see the seething masses and when I looked back, he had gone. I don't mind telling you I was scared and couldn't wait to leave. The only thing missing was the 'Mark of the Beast 666.' I conclude that this seems to be a many-layered movement incorporating groups of white supremacists across the world. We have got close to identifying some of them but now, for the first time I heard reference to an all—powerful 'Leader,' and to Europe. Was this a coincidence or did 'The Chief' let a cat out of the bag? Perhaps there's more to this than meets the eye.'

End of report. Signed Zeb Clowsky.

After Reuben and his committee had read this it was destroyed. 'Far too dangerous to have around,' said Reuben, 'and I only hope that Zeb got away with it as he thinks he did. Otherwise he might be tracked to us.'

As it turned out he was right and it wasn't long before we had visitors asking for Mr Solidar. Reuben appeared at once and ushered them out of the flat, down the stairs and into the neighbouring park. 'You'd better say what you've got to say here,' he said, 'I don't want you upsetting my friends.' There were two men, one short and one tall. The short one spoke first. 'So you know who we are then?' he enquired. At first Reuben was inclined to say yes but then he realised that that might be the more dangerous option. 'Actually, no I don't but I suppose it's about this internment business with the Shu's. Whoever you are just leave us alone.' Now the tall one spoke. 'That's good. We don't want anybody interfering in our business either. So we understand one another?' Reuben nodded and, with nothing more said, the men moved away. Reuben now realised he could no longer stay at the flat so, despite my pleas, he left and took up residence in the Wilmington Hotel off Long Beach.

*   *   *   *

Now KoKo picked up the story again. 'And that's the last we saw of him, until the police called and said they had found two bodies washed up on the beach, one was Zeb Clowsky and the other was Reuben. And now you're here we can organise a second post mortem on Cecil's authority.'

Jed spoke up softly and with some feeling, 'Well we can't bring him back but we can try to get some justice for him and for Zeb of course as well as the whole JA community. I'd like to suggest that, in addition to the post mortem that we look in to Zeb's movements and contacts. Then we should pay a visit to Tule Lake for some stories and photos. I have a feeling that we won't be very welcome there. Lastly I suggest some on the street interviews with families being evicted. All good copy.'

Akiro and Kojiro nodded their approval, so for the next few days and weeks they followed the plan. The independent coroner confirmed that both Zeb and Reuben had been expertly stabbed and then 'roughed up' to hide their injuries. The report added that Reuben's body had what he termed 'a rather recent tattoo' with the letters AAL that he took to be some girl friend's initials. Although he was not hopeful Jed took his findings to the local police. 'Ah yes,' said the officer in charge

'Nasty business, now what can I do to help? Seems like a fight that went wrong. No witnesses, and to be honest it seems like they were looking for trouble. Well I'll do what I can of course but I strongly advise you to leave well alone now. We don't want any more unfortunate incidents do we? I hope I'm making myself clear.' And with that he placed the file in the Non Urgent tray. Jed was disappointed but as he turned to leave he noticed that the officer winked knowingly at a colleague, and it was only then that Jed spotted the initials on his knuckles. They were ALL. He knew now that he and Gina only had a limited time to complete their work before they might be added to the 'casualty' list.

Fortunately the other parts of his plan went very well with much publicity for the plight of the AJ community and some changes were made as a result to their conditions, both in the internment camp and regarding periods of notice of eviction etc. They also picked up some clues about 'The Chief' having not only connections with drug money but a highly legitimate presence in commerce, on Wall Street and in Washington as well. Details were however too sketchy to mean much at this stage, and as for 'The Leader' that Zeb had mentioned, Jed realised that they would have to follow that one up back in LA to see if it actually meant anything.

It was time to leave. They had done what they came for, although they wished that they had achieved more. Now they must bid 'Sayonara' to Kojiro and Akiro, and this was quite a tearful occasion especially for Akiro as she had become very fond of Gina especially. 'Sayonara!' she called from her balcony, as she waved a tiny hanky and dropped flower blossom over the parapet in their path. 'Sayonara, byee.'

On their return to New York Jed&Gina made an appointment to see Cecil the very next day and he greeted them with a smile when they knocked on the door. 'My friends, my friends,' he said, 'Good to see you, I've just been playing 'Ghost of a Chance,' I'd almost forgotten how good it was.'

Saying this he sat back and waited as Jed nodded to Gina to give him the details of their visit to LA. When she had finished he just smiled and said, 'Just as I thought, just as I thought but thank you, thank you so much. I feel that I can put Reuben's memory to rest now.' Jed said, 'I wish that we could have done more but there are some loose ends we'll be tying up and we'll come back to see you soon.' Gina then went over to Cecil and bent down to give him a kiss. He flushed and said, 'Oh dear I'm sure I've done nothing to deserve that, but it was very nice just the same. Now wait there a moment, I want to give something to Jed.'

He stood up and briefly left the room returning with a small package. 'Here,' he said, 'this is for you.' Gina took the parcel and, turning to Jed she said 'Shall we?' He nodded and they carefully undid a pretty ribbon and peeled back some brown paper to reveal a small box.

Gina opened the lid gently and there within was an embossed medal with the words, 'To Reuben Solidar for selfless devotion to others.' On the back were the initials NAACP 1942. Jed spoke up quickly, 'I can't take this, really I can't, it's too precious and we know how you loved him so.' However Cecil put his hand up, as a policeman would on traffic duty and said, 'No, just hear me out. People thought that Reuben was a great musician and he was, but for him the most important thing was the fate and welfare of others less fortunate than himself. He knew that his work was dangerous but it did not deter him and he tried to protect me. I want you to have the medal because I know that you will continue his work and I will always have his music. Now, leave me before I cry again, please.' He turned to the old record player and once more the strains of 'Ghost of a Chance' began to fill the room but he did not turn around. Jed&Gina tiptoed out quietly and as Jed looked at her he could see that she was crying too, but so was he. The next morning it all began again. Somehow the Honey got into the Arts section in the newspaper, and after much gentle 'surgery' to prise the pages apart, the effort was finally abandoned. 'How would you like Jam instead?' asked Jed 'Now what do you think Cecil meant yesterday when he said that 'he knew that I would continue the work' 'Exactly what he said, and I agree with him. It's like a baton that has been passed on. One warrior has died and now you must pick it up and run with it wherever it takes you.' she said. 'Yes,' he replied 'but this whole business may not be as simple as it seems. In other words, white supremacy in the States goes way back and persecutions of minorities, especially Jews in Europe does also but what a toxic mix it would be if disparate groups throughout the world got really organised.' Gina thought for a moment then replied.

'That's your task then, to see if it is so. You must seek out the mysterious 'Leader' and the organisation that surrounds him. You must check all avenues where power may be exerted, in Politics, in Business, in the Military, yes and even in Religion and you can't rest until it's done.'

Now Jed was beginning to wonder what he had let himself in for as two other thoughts came to mind. 'Gina' he said 'We'd better get used to the fact that I'm not going to be around much longer because I'm bound to get my draft papers soon. Heaven knows where I'll end up and I'd be really worried about you if you started 'making waves.' Gina moved to sit beside him and held his hand. 'I didn't know that you cared but I love you Jedsy Lomax,' she said, 'and we could be a good a team. If you promise that you'll take care of yourself for me I'll do the same for you.' He stroked her hand, 'I promise,' he said. 'I know now that I love you Gina, don't worry, I'll be back soon and we'll be together again.'

End Of Part One

PART TWO
'SENTIMENTAL JOURNEY.'

The Draft cometh

The attack on Pearl Harbour on December 7th 1941 had set the wheels in motion for draft papers to be issued to those eligible to join the armed forces. Fortunately Jed had not received his in the first months, so he had been able to go to LA to investigate Reuben's death and help out with Billy Shu and the problems caused by the Japanese internments. However it was now August '42 and at last the long-awaited envelope popped through the letter-box. Jed looked at Gina (who seemed to have become a permanent fixture) and she looked back. Neither moved for what seemed like ages as they sat either side of the breakfast table laid out as usual with cereals, toast and honey of course. Jed moved his hand across the table to hers and that was the last straw as she bent forward to kiss his hand in a flood of tears. She gripped so tightly that it hurt with her nails digging in and drawing blood. He waited for some time until her grip relaxed and then, removing his hand very gently, he said, 'Better go and see darling.' It had been so long in coming that Jed was actually relieved so he strode to the door with some purpose, picking up the envelope and bringing it back to the table. He picked up a knife from the table. Unfortunately it was the honey knife and as usual it tended to 'gum up the works.' As Jed struggled with the sticky envelope Gina reached over the table. 'Here let me do it' she said with a smile and then she was laughing and crying all at the same time. 'Thanks Gina' he said, 'Ah, here it is. Report for two month's training next week, somewhere near Boston. But look, why don't we have a real break from it all now and have a sunshine break in Santa Monica before I get any orders to join a regiment. They usually give you some embarkation leave. What do you think?' 'Deal.' she said, 'but only if you promise not to get hurt if you do have to go overseas.' 'Agreed' Jed replied, 'I'm no hero. They'll probably give me an office job back so I should be quite safe.' 'And I'll be getting on with some research while you're away if you like.' she said, not wishing to seem too pushy. She had noticed that he could be nervous if she got too close, but she also felt that he was growing to love her. 'Seems like a good idea' he replied, 'but let's get on with our packing, I thought we'd try to get in at the Georgian Hotel near the pier. It's very traditional but modernised of course. I'm sure that you'll love it.' Gina wondered who he had been with that last time but she thought it best not to enquire. This was to be 'their' weekend and she would allow nothing to spoil it. 'Nightie or no nightie?' she called cheekily from the bedroom and waited for his reply. At last it came. 'Well it can be very hot there.' he said.

Santa Monica

'The Georgian Hotel' is situated at 1415 Ocean Avenue in Santa Monica directly facing the beach and only a short distance from the Pier and the 'world famous' Big Dean's Ocean Front Café. It's rather a diminutive building standing between more modern and taller hotels but charm it certainly has. First there's the colour scheme for the facade, a unique blend of 'sea blue' with orange and yellow accessories, making it stand out amongst all the other buildings of stone. Secondly there's the veranda facing the beach, a place to sit and watch, or dine of course. Last but by no means least is it's history, and it was this that Jed wanted to share with Gina as it had a somewhat romantic, as well as a dubious past.

First though, having booked in, it was time for a stroll in the sunshine around this 'Bayside District' which encompassed palm trees in Palisades Park, parrots on the pier and promenades, avenues and boulevards with names such as Broadway (not THE Broadway), Wilshire, Pico and Colorado amongst others. There are also link roads, handily called Second, Third and Fourth Streets and it was here, amongst some itinerant musicians and very helpful 'Santa Monica Town Guides,' some on a sort of scooter cycle, that Jed and Gina walked hand in hand until dusk.

Back at the hotel they sat at a small table on the veranda overlooking the Pacific Ocean as the sun went down. 'Do you know,' said Gina, 'I don't think that you could have picked a more beautiful place. Everything about it is, well, rather romantic don't you think?' This was the chance that Jed had been waiting for, a chance to lend real substance to Gina's romantic notions but he began carefully, planning to warm up to his main revelation after a few more drinks and when it was time to turn in.

'I'm glad you think it's a good choice. Of course LA proper is only about 20 minutes drive away using the Pacific Coast Highway and you can pop into the Getty museum and take in Hollywood as well. But I agree with you. It seems to be quieter here and not so rushed. Did I tell you that this hotel was built in 1933 when California was really growing and it was the first hotel on the 'front'. All these others came later. They called it 'The Lady' back then, after the owner's mother who probably kept an eye on things. The restaurant was one of the last strongholds of the 'prohibition era,' a 'speakeasy' of sorts until gamblers and drinkers found it easier to take a motorboat offshore to one of the many 'casino barges' in the Bay.'

Jed sensed that soon it would be time to divulge his little secret but he thought he might tease Gina just a bit. 'I suppose the gangsters kept everyone away don't you? I suppose they liked it nice and quiet like us don't you think?' Gina was looking out to sea rather wistfully and didn't reply so Jed decided to play his trump card. But had he left it too late?

'Gina, Gina. Look at me Gina. Now just guess whose room we'll be in tonight?' She looked startled. 'Room? Our room I should hope.' she replied looking a bit bemused. 'Yes, yes but who else has used the room?' he continued. 'Plenty I suppose.' she said. 'I don't think I follow you. Sorry I must be tired. Do go on. Tell me.' Jed was relieved, he'd nearly blown it and now here it was, his special secret. 'Clarke Gable and Carole Lombard that's who, yes we'll be using the bed that they slept in. Now what do you think of that?' Now Gina was looking at him in a different way, her eyelids half closed, not from sleep but from an imaginary smoke haze. She pursed her lips and touched her cheek with one finger of her right hand. 'Shall we go and see then?' she murmured rather huskily. 'Wow' thought Jed, 'She's playing the part already.' He smiled and took her hand, 'Here's looking at you kid' he said fully realising that he had Bogart's line, but what the hell. The lift was one of those old kinds with the double cage doors but the bedroom had been modernised to include a bathroom and Gina was soon in the shower. Jed waited patiently until she came out dressed only in a towelling robe. She smiled that mysterious Lombard/Bacall smile and just said, 'Which side Clark?' This was his moment, the moment he had been waiting for and he delivered his line in laconic Gable style, 'Frankly my dear' he said, 'I don't give a damn.' His actions however belied that sentiment as he leaned across and nuzzled her damp hair.

'Wish me luck'

The week had week flashed by, one of those very special weeks heightened by the drama that they knew was to come, and now it was time for Jed to report for training. This time Gina was more composed because she did not want to upset him, so she suggested that they said goodbye at his flat when the taxi came. She didn't think that she could remain calm if she went to the railway station and so it was done, with a big kiss, a hug and a wave. Now she could cry.

Pepper pots and fruit

Eight weeks loomed before her so she decided to get busy on some issues that had been bothering her since Reuben's death. She and Jed had already decided that Cecil's contacts in the world of music might reap some results but this could wait for now. A thought was nagging at her that all the answers were not to be found there nor even in the USA alone. It was self evident that the KKK and associated parties were alive and well in America, especially in the Southern States, targeting the Negro as inferior and expendable (except for labour of course) but Reuben had died for the Japanese residents who had also been singled out for 'special treatment.' Furthermore Reuben and Cecil had been made aware of malevolent anti Semitic forces at work in Europe during their tours. 'Maybe this is just the way of the world' she thought, 'but what if, what if some or all of these groups got together? What we've seen so far could then prove to be the tip of a very deep and dangerous iceberg.'

With this in mind she decided to play a 'what if' game with herself on the lounge floor with various objects that came to hand. First a large old tablecloth that she turned into a map of the world and then some characters to inhabit the space. First she populated the US with Jed's figurines from the Civil War, naming them in turn Government, Commerce, Industry and Church. Who else but these could mastermind any plan across the world, let alone State Borders? Next she populated the UK with the same titles, this time in the guise of salt and pepper pots but she also added a third, a pepper grinder in fact, to represent Royalty. In Europe and the Far East she decided on coloured pencils in wine glasses to demonstrate fascist (black) communist (red) and democratic (green) with 5 pencils of one colour denoting total control, and, say 2 for moderate. A fourth colour, yellow would denote neutral. She decided that she did not know enough about South America to be certain, but she had heard that some countries had fascist sympathies so Brazil, for example, warranted a single black pencil and Argentina two.

Now, would it be appropriate or necessary to include a religious dimension? Might it be said, for example that some doctrines were more likely to be supportive of anti-Semitic and racist groups than others? Once more she could not be sure but decided to err on the side of inclusion rather than the opposite. For her purposes a broad split between East and West would suffice. She did not think that Sunni and Shia Islam could be termed racist (although they were hostile) or that Shinto and Buddhism were either, nor Hindus and Moslems although they were inevitably antagonistic. Judaism was central of course but the Jews did not have a State (Israel was founded post war) but the main one that came to mind was the support given by the Roman Catholic Church to Fascism as in the Spanish Civil War, and the lack of action by the Holy See in Rome in the face of the constant harassment of the

Jews, not to mention proven tales of mass executions of the innocent ignored. (See Notes)

There were warm words sometimes and even a little help here and there, but no outright and categorical condemnation of the whole system.

Even in the USA she remembered how Father Coughlin (The father of Hate radio) had used his station from the mid 1930's to reach more than 40 million people. By 1939 he was directing the 'Christian Front' in league with the German American Bund. So, yes, she would place religion squarely on the map as being potentially implicated in racial affairs, sometimes as an onlooker or bystander but also as a participant.

She looked around for some demarcation objects but finding none she had to settle for fruit. There were red and white grapes, apples, pears, oranges, apricots and even Kiwis that were added to the map. She laughed at the display and hoped that she would not have visitors.

It was finished. The scene was set. The actors were on stage so what now? Well, her back ached and it was time for a stiff drink, a 'screwdriver' to be precise which she mixed and downed in one. Next she sat thoughtfully in her favourite chair and surveyed her handiwork. She held a writing pad on her lap and began to write. The first words that spilled out on to the page were those old favourites, who, what, why, when and how. Then she rearranged them from the easiest to the hardest. She already had some clues as to the what, and how, but why, when and most importantly WHO were still a mystery. She stared at the words in disbelief. Yes she had cracked it. Not the answers but the Questions. Now all she had to do was to match these with her scenario on the floor and surely some connections would materialise. She thought that Jed would be very pleased with her. How she missed him, especially as she lay alone that night reaching out with a sigh, only to hold her pillow tight.

The next morning she looked proudly at her handiwork. The pepper grinder commanded her attention probably because it was the largest object on the table. Mmmm, royal avenues or blind alleys she wondered. Her characters were coming to life. Firstly there was Mr and Mrs Simpson and the Duke of Windsor at the 'Fort' in pre war days, as well as her 'friendship' with Count Ciano, Mussolini's foreign minister. These murky waters had now been muddied even more by the mysterious Duke of Hamilton and the flight of Rudolph Hess to Scotland in 1941 to meet a 'Duke,' but which one? Was it Hamilton as was alleged, or the Duke of Windsor himself, known to have Nazi sympathies or, even more extraordinary, it had even been rumoured that the Duke of Kent had been there in 1941.

Author's note (*He was later killed in 'another' flight over Scotland in 1942. Connections, if any, remain shrouded in mystery*)

So, what clues were there that might implicate a shipping magnate from the USA (Simpson) with links to British Royalty, an American hero with Fascist sympathies (Charles Lindbergh), a charismatic American Roman Catholic priest (Coughlin) with Mafia bosses such as Luciano and Gambini, as well as leaders of the KKK and ALL (American Liberty League). Even more importantly was there a connection between any or all of these with the Fascist plan for the racial domination of the world that was already under way in Europe? It struck Gina, as it had done Jed earlier, that should such malevolent forces come together with proper organisation and commitment then the outlook was very bleak indeed.

She wasn't at all sure, but thought that finding connections would be a good place to start her research anyway, because she was aiming to uncover the covert side of any conspiracy that might exist. Reuben's experiences and those of Cecil might well inform the overt side, the what, why, when and even the how but she was after the WHO. Reuben Solidar's experiences in the world of show business and elsewhere had convinced him that there were indeed connections. In his eyes it was 'Whitey' against the rest, be they Black, Asiatic or any other colour. It also seemed that those who feared communism cast their net wide and saw these minority groups as seditious, especially in the USA. She remembered that he had told her of Father Coughlin's plan to invade Mexico in the cause of religion. True or not it demonstrated to her that there were, at this time, no boundaries for those who would seek a new world order and a white Anglo Saxon hegemony.

She wrote two large words on her pad with a question mark. They were 'COMMON CAUSE,' but she knew she must dig much deeper if she was to expose this. Then she added a third, 'LEADER' that mysterious figure that kept appearing and disappearing just as fast. She knew that she must eliminate the innocent in order to close in on the guilty so her first job tomorrow then was to go to the library and dig up all she could about the Simpsons and their business and political world, rather than the romantic one covered by so many journalists. Simpson owned a shipping line and that gave him world-wide access to important business figures and diplomats across the world. Not only that, but shipping also opened up remote corners of the globe in which resources necessary for any future hostile action might be hidden away, she thought, but maybe that was just too fanciful. Next job was to trawl any press cuttings about the Hess affair to see if that had been another potential 'cornerstone of common cause,' albeit nipped in the bud. Then, she thought, 'I'll do a check on Coughlin, he had the ear of many powerful 'players' in politics, church and the Mafia. He's next.'

A nasty surprise

The next day Gina was up and about early in Jed's flat sorting out papers for her research when there was a knock at the door. She hoped it wasn't visitors because it was in the flat that she had spread out her tablecloth and map of the world. Although she had her own place, she liked to be in his flat when he was away. Somehow it made her feel closer to him.

Nevertheless she was quite cautious about opening the door, making sure that the security chain was firmly in place. She was therefore able initially to peek through the small viewing aperture before she had to make a decision to open or not. She squinted through the small space and what she saw caused her to gasp in apprehension. Two uniformed officers of the Marine Corps stood on the doorstep holding their ID cards up in front of them. She noted that they were a man and a woman and their badges declared them to be Captain Walcot and Lieutenant Morrell.

'We are very sorry to disturb you,' said the man, 'but may we come in please. We wish to speak to Mrs Lomax.' Gina bit her lip until it bled. She could only imagine the worst so, as if in a daze, she opened the door and said, 'Yes, please come in, I'm afraid you startled me for a moment.'

She stood back and beckoned them into the lounge, which was of course, dominated by her display. 'Please be careful' she said, 'please excuse the mess. Perhaps we can sit over here by the window.' The two officers followed and sat down before the woman spoke. 'I'm Captain Walcot and this is Lieutenant Morrell. Are you Mrs Lomax?' Once more Gina felt awkward, 'Well no as a matter of fact, I'm Gina Lombardi and Jed and I, well we're very good friends, if you see what I mean.' There followed a rather embarrassing pause as the two officers looked at one another before the Captain continued. 'I'm sorry to tell you then Gina that we are not authorised to discuss this matter with you and apologise for disturbing you at this hour.' Saying which she closed her case and made to stand up.

'No. No.' Gina cried out, 'You must tell me, you must. I must know if something dreadful has happened. I really must. Tell me, please tell me.'

Once more the officer exchanged glance before the Lieutenant spoke, 'To be quite honest Gina we should have checked next of kin before we came to this address. Don't you think it's only fair to tell Gina now and catch up with others later?' Hearing this Gina suddenly lost all control of her knees and slumped to the floor, her face as white as a sheet. Seeing this the Captain spoke up quickly, 'Yes you are right Lieutenant. Gina, Gina, listen to me. Jed is only injured not dead, that is what we have come to tell his loved ones and I can see that you are one of them. Lieutenant, please get a glass of water for the lady.' Now the Captain took hold of Gina's arm and helped her into a chair as the Lieutenant returned with the water. 'Here, drink this,' he said sympathetically, 'You'll feel better in a moment.' Gina took the glass and suddenly the two officers came into focus again. 'Tell me' she repeated, 'Tell me what happened please.' Now it was the Captain who spoke again, 'The fact is Gina,' she said, 'that Jed has been badly wounded during practice for an amphibious landing. He's out of danger now but he is seriously hurt and may lose an arm. That's all I can say at present.' 'Thank God, thank God!' Gina cried out, moving automatically to hug the Captain who held her warmly for a few moments as she explained, 'He's in Mount Vernon hospital at the moment and if you ring you may be able to visit. As you're not a relative I advise you to use this code, 'Vista'. That should get you in, meanwhile can you confirm the address of Jed's parents to check with our records, we need to get in touch with them of course so please don't phone Jed until tomorrow by which time we will have spoken to them.'

With that, the two officers left and Gina was left alone and the tears began again as she sat looking at her map which she could hardly see for the blur in her eyes. What would have been the point of all this if Jed had been killed she thought, but she also knew the answer. Like Reuben and Cecil she knew that the job had to be finished, She could only hope and pray that Jed would come home well enough to carry on, and on the bright side he might not have to serve overseas after all.

Gina was like a cat on a hot tin roof all night. She seemed to look at the clock every half hour as the night dragged on. She must have fallen asleep eventually because when she next looked it was 9am and she'd had enough waiting. Gingerly she picked up the phone and dialled the hospital number that had been given to her expecting to have to go through receptionists, ward sisters and the like but no, the voice she heard was Jed's, wonderful lovely, wonderful Jed. 'Hello.' the voice said, 'this is Lieutenant Lomax. Who's speaking please?'

Gina was so excited she couldn't think what to say but finally she blurted it out. 'Jed, it's me Gina, your Gina. It's so good to hear your voice.'

'And yours my darling,' he replied, 'I suppose you've heard that I've been a bit careless, but I think I'm on the mend. It's a great hospital.'

'But your arm, they said it was quite bad, please tell me. Does it hurt?'

'No not really, I suppose I'm drugged up a bit and these doctors always make it sound worse than it is. When can you come up to see me?'

'As soon as I can get there. I'm dashing out of the door right now in my mind but I suppose it'll have to be tomorrow. I've missed you so much. At least I might have you home for a while.'

'OK see you then and yes you might have me around for quite a while.'

With that Gina put the phone down with a sigh of relief. Suddenly she felt very tired and it promised to be a busy day tomorrow.

Back home

Visits came and went over the next few weeks and soon Jed was back home, arm in a sling but saved. He joked that he looked like Wingy Manone the 1930's trumpeter from New Orleans who had lost an arm in a streetcar accident at an early age but had gone on to lead some very good and indeed popular bands of the era

(Author's note. *Joe Manone was born in 1904 of Italian parents and had a smash hit juke box success in 1935 with 'The Isle of Capri'. Later he was given carte blanche to choose his own musicians and they were often amongst the best including Chu Berry, Buster Bailey, Cozy Cole, Matty Matlock, Joe Marsala, George Brunis, Eddie Miller and others.*)

When he first saw Gina's display he laughed out loud saying that it reminded him of an Alice in Wonderland picnic, but he had to admit that it was a rather useful way of visualising what they were up against.

'You've done a wonderful job,' he said, 'but I rather think that there are four ingredients missing that just might have a role to play. I'm not saying that they do, but they just might.

Firstly I'm thinking of the Masons who, as you know operate just about everywhere. Such an organisation could provide very useful bases in far away areas as well as in major conurbations. I visited Queenstown, deep in the remote South Island of New Zealand awhile back and there, tucked rather anonymously on the bay was a Masonic Lodge. Probably quite innocent I suppose but not far away from Doubtful Sound, which must be one of the most isolated areas in the world, yet with access to the sea.

Secondly there's the Military. Not only here and in Europe, but the potential is there for collusion in a number of areas. We've seen what can happen with the Axis forces of Germany, Italy and Japan and potentially with the League of Nations if that organisation fell into the wrong hands.

Thirdly let's consider oil. The stuff that makes the world go round and without which any attempt at a new world order would soon founder. Remember that Hitler's interest in venturing east is not just for 'liebensraum' (living space) but also for resources, including oil.

So, if there is a plan, long in the making, to bring together strands of a white racist hegemony across the globe, it could not be done without 'liquid gold' and planners would need to make sure that supplies would be available worldwide and that means control over the Middle East, probably through financial muscle rather than military might.

Fifthly it's the money. Who might be prepared to bankroll the whole affair? 'Follow the money' they say, and if we start from the bottom up we might get somewhere and we probably do have some data on this.'

Gina looked somewhat crestfallen at his additions to her tablecloth but smiled just the same. 'Well let's hope we've got it all covered from A-Z' she said, 'but I've got a feeling that we're overcooking the omelette. Remember that Reuben's personal experience was rather limited. I don't think that he really considered this wider scenario do you?' Jed thought for a moment and now he seemed somewhat downcast. 'You're right of course. Let's stick to what we know and if it leads elsewhere so well and good, we will have carried out Reuben's 'legacy.' Agreed?' Gina smiled, 'Agreed.' she said, 'Now how about some fun if your arm is up to it.'

The Dynamic Dorseys

The next morning Gina reminded Jed that Cecil would be appearing with Jimmy Dorsey at the Trocadero the next day and that they had promised to go. 'Yes,' Jed agreed, 'and maybe he's had his nose to the ground as well. That new promoter wants watching I've heard.' Cecil was not a renowned soloist like his brother Reuben but he was well respected as a useful player in the trombone sections of a number of different outfits.

Jimmy Dorsey was a virtuoso clarinettist and alto saxophonist and, like his brother Tommy he led very successful bands during the 1930's and 1940's. They had even ventured a band together (The Dorsey Brothers) before falling out in 1935 when Tommy walked out of the Glen Island Casino. Jimmy replaced him on trombone with Bobby Byrne and began to use Cecil as a dep. (Author's note 1) *The Dorsey Brothers were reunited in 1953)*). Meanwhile Jimmy's band benefited from the vocals of Bob Eberly and Helen O'Connell as well as sidemen such as Ray McKinlay on drums. They had 'hits' including Anapola, Blue Eyes and Tangerine but some said that the band could not decide whether to be a large Dixieland group (such as Bob Crosby) or settle on smooth swing. Given their 'hit records' it was obvious the way the wind was blowing.

(Note 2) *Eberly was drafted in 1943 and Kitty Kallen replaced Helen)*

Jimmy always made sure that his sidemen got the best of everything and on this occasion they all had rooms at the Viceroy Hotel, and it was there that Jed and Gina joined him after the concert. 'Great session' said Gina, 'Jimmy's certainly got the band moving together hasn't he?' Cecil smiled, 'I guess you could say that,' he said, 'but it's no holiday. If it's not just so in rehearsal we have to do it again and again.' 'Sounds like Tommy, or BG (Goodman) for that matter.' replied Jed, 'It's all in the name of good music, and the 'Hit Parade' of course,' Cecil nodded his agreement and passed G&T's around before taking a seat. 'Now, what would you like to know?' he said. 'The same as usual,' replied Jed, 'Reuben thought that he was onto something and it probably cost him his life. Let's put it this way. He left us with traces or hints rather than substantive evidence that, not only was racism endemic in society but, if not exposed in the dark corners where it thrives, public political protestations will have no effect. And anyway, who in the Deep South would speak out against the Klan and it's supporters? So, as I see it our job is to shed a little light in the world of showbiz you might say, and maybe that will lead to other revelations in due course. Now, where to begin? Might I suggest Cecil that you tell us what it's like to be on the road with the Dorsey band, and maybe the others in due time. But for now let's concentrate on one tour, this band, this leader and this agent. It's quite likely I think that it's the agents who call the shots and maybe set certain economic (racist) criteria for non-white musicians. Right?'

'You sure are.' replied Cecil, 'but it's always been that way, and, as you say, especially down in the Southern States. Jim Crow, him alive and well down dere.' Cecil finished his sentence with a smile at his own joke. 'Yes Cecil,' added Gina, 'but we're up here not down dere, as you put it.'

'OK,' said Cecil, 'Let me take you through the situation here and now in the Dorsey band. Jimmy is a great leader and sax player. He's also very fair-minded and I've never seen him show any racism. He admires Johnny Hodges and Benny Carter too much to even consider it but even he can come under pressure from agents when they offer work. Last month in fact I'd heard that Jimmy had offered a chair to Frankie Parkes, that new Creole reedman from New Orleans. Apparently it was almost sealed and delivered when, according to Jimmy, he was taken to one side by Bruno Morton the agent, that 'they' meaning him or others maybe, preferred young Tad Laker from Boston, a fine player it's true, and white of course. You never can get at the motivations you see. And on top of this, Jimmy told me, Rudy Gilbert the manager at the Trocadero had been promised an award for 'Services to the Real America' by another group not known to me. The award was conditional on customer turnout on the tour especially in the South, where blacks were not welcome in white bands, although Artie Shaw and others have tried to break this taboo'

Jed pricked up his ears, 'Do you know Cecil I think that you may have given us our first big lead. This 'Services to the Real America' sounds suspiciously like the 'ALL' group that we've come across before, albeit in a different guise. If awards are given here, no doubt there are awards elsewhere and what better way of directing, or let's say 'influencing' matters in the right (ie racist) direction. It could also serve to construct a 'black' list, if you'll excuse the pun, now you must be tired and we'll leave you alone. Tomorrow Gina and I can do some research into the awards to see if they are widespread and even more important, see if there's a money trail. That would be a real bonus.'

'I can't Jed,' said Gina, 'I just can't. Marie phoned last night and said that Mama and Papa had been 'detained' for questioning in Rome. I'm worried sick.' Jed took her hand tenderly, 'No, of course not,' he said, 'How selfish of me. I'll make a start and you catch up if you can later.

I know someone in the US delegation over there if it might be any help.'

She was somewhat comforted and said, 'Yes Jed, would you, please, maybe they can find out something.'

The STRA Awards

Jed sniffed progress. He soon found out that the STRA awards were not uncommon at all nor were they localised. Trawls through the records in the Library soon revealed that such awards had been given to a mother's group in Dallas, a school in Columbus, a medical centre in Selma and even a Boy's Brigade in Boston. All were reported as being 'successful' and in one case, a publishers in Pittsburgh, there was an award of $2500 for 'services' countersigned 'Parry for H.' What did all this mean? Were these disparate groups all part of a network of 'sleeper' cells waiting to be activated or were some of them just innocent activities being used as cover by a wider group? The more he found the more Jed enthused. He was like a bloodhound within a 'whiff' if not a sight of his quarry, but he was missing Gina. He missed her good sense, but above all he missed the warmth that she seemed to exude, oh how he missed that.

His head was buried deep in some old files when he sensed that very warmth close by and, turning around he saw her. Yes there she was with a big smile. 'They're out!' she exclaimed, 'they've been released. Papa just phoned, they're out!' Jed stood up and took her in his arms, 'Thank God, thank God' he said. He knew how easily she might crumble in adversity. She didn't seem to have his knack of 'bounce back' at least not in the short term. 'They're moving on to Florence,' she said, 'possibly a bit safer there, if anywhere is so I'll just have to pray for them'. Jed thought it strange that he'd been calling on God to help and now here she was praying when neither of them had much time for formalised religion.

There was no getting away from it though, there was something there and it wasn't just spirituality. It was more concrete than that. It was as if a light touch was watching over them, one might even say a Guardian Angel perhaps. 'But who believes in Angels?' he thought.

Now Gina became businesslike once more. 'You seem to have done a lot of work but to be honest we know nothing for sure,' she said, 'so there are awards, so what, we don't have any idea if they are connected, other than winning an award do we?'

But Jed smiled with a look of certainty on his face, 'You're forgetting about the money my sweet. Who is the paymaster and why, and what 'services' were referred to at the publishers? Let's phone them using undercover pseudonyms of course. Let's say we're the Bank and ask about the 'cheque' for the award. We might get lucky and get the signatories or, if it was cash, well we might get a lead as to the donor. Then we do it all over again with as many recipients of the award as we can find. Let's find out if there's a 'smoking gun' and who's pointing it at whom.' When he finished this little speech he looked quite flushed and Gina was a bit worried that he might be overdoing it. 'Take it easy,' she said, 'the problem will still be here in the morning. Remember the doctors said you had to be careful for a while. You've had a shock to your system with the injury and you need to slow down a bit. Let's have an early night and I'll start another trawl in the morning while you sleep in. Deal?'

Jed knew that it was no use arguing and he knew that she was right, and maybe there could be benefits from an early night. 'Deal.' he said.

The next day Gina put together a copious list of STRA award winners and then took Jed his breakfast in bed. He was grateful to have had a sleep in but also anxious to make progress. 'How did you get on?' he said. 'I've done the list,' replied Gina, 'now I'm going to make some phone calls. I'll make a call to some of these to start with and just say that I'm from the STRA awards office and that we are updating our records.

I'll say that 'our' awards are funded in different ways and we just wanted to check which of 'our offices' made the payment to them. OK. Let's say it was Chicago. Then we ask to confirm the cheque signatories, for example, was it Innes&Bradley. No? And who is H please? Hopefully names would be given. Oh. It was cash. Never mind, do you have the signed donation slip? Thank you and sorry to trouble you.' She finished with a smile and said, 'what do you think Jed?'

He looked at her with some admiration and said, 'Well I never took you to be a natural con-artist but if anyone can carry this off, you can. Good luck and by the way have you thought of a name?' 'I have,' she replied, 'but don't laugh, it's Miss Dolores Dimm. I thought that this would give the impression that I'm a teeny bit slow, maybe a bit inefficient, hence the enquiry.' Jed sank back into his pillows with a sigh, 'Well you'd better get on with it Miss Dimm' he said, 'I'm for some more shut eye.' and he was asleep again in seconds as Gina tiptoed out of the room.

Cecil on Tour

Meanwhile Cecil had begun a series of engagements countrywide with a fair few of the top bands going. Strangely he was not one of those players like Harry Carney with the 'Duke' or Freddy Green with the 'Count' who stuck to one band. Actually as 'dep' he was paid rather more because of the general inconvenience of unexpected and short notice travel etc. all in all it suited him and, after the Dorsey engagement he had hurried off to join Les Brown and his 'Band of Renown' on tour in Boston, Baltimore, New York and Washington. Jed had asked him to keep his eyes open and to telegraph names of agents and any issues concerning racial prejudice that he came across. Also he was to look out for more STRA connections if there were any. Might he be able to find out who was paying these large amounts?

The 'Band of Renown'

Les Brown was another alto player but he rarely took solos. It might be said that his instrument was his band and he was more successful than most with hits such as 'Bizet had his day' and 'Mexican hat dance.'

Author's note (*A young singer named Doris Day joined in 1940 and went on to record Brown's greatest hit 'Sentimental Journey' in 1945.*)

It was not a star-studded outfit but it did include brilliant arrangements from Frank Comstock and the ebullient Ted Nash on sax. The band featured six trombones so it was not unusual for Cecil to dep for one of them. On this occasion it was 'Stumpy' Brown. Cecil kept in touch with Jed as promised through the telegraph system providing a number of amusing tales but more importantly a few names.

George Ganton was 'the' impresario in that part of the world and Cecil reported that nothing went on during the tour without his say so. On two occasions it was rumoured that concert seats had been given away to white followers rather than sold to blacks who applied and who would have paid. The method used was to accept provisional bookings from the black community on the understanding that seats 'may or may not' be available. Nevertheless a deposit had to be paid and this was not refundable. As the date of the concert approached and seats still remained these were 'donated' by an organisation called 'LOS or Lovers of Swing' to selected 'deserving' citizens. The black community were told that all seats had been 'taken' and of course, they lost their deposit. There was no fuss because not many people knew how or why it was done. As promised, Cecil reported all this back to Jed before he set off for Florida.

'Mad Mab' Barnet

Cecil's next stint was with the Charlie Barnet Band on a tour of Florida. (It is said that Charlie got the nickname from one of his many wives.)

Unusually he often led his band from Soprano sax but he also played alto and tenor and by 1933 he was leading a band that included the celebrated arranger and trumpeter Eddie Sauter. In 1936 he tried his luck in the movies in Hollywood appearing in such films as 'Love and Hisses.' However he was soon back at the front of his band appearing at many prestigious venues including the Glen Island Casino, the Paramount and the 'Famous Door.' This was all going well until 1939 when a mysterious fire burnt down the Palomar Hotel in Los Angeles destroying all band manuscripts and instruments. Band solidarity was quickly shown when Duke Ellington replaced them all, and the band recovered well enough to record a hit with 'Cherokee' arranged by Billy May.

(Author's note. *His biggest 'hit' came later in 1944 with Skyliner.*)

An investigation into the fire failed to find the culprits but arson was suspected especially as documents found at the scene were found to be a plan of the theatre with indications as to where timing devices might be placed. Faded signatures seemed to be LDR/HYD but no one could suggest what these might mean. The possibility that the fire was aimed specifically at the Barnet band cannot be ignored because, like Artie Shaw 'Mad Mab' had insisted on hiring the best musicians that he could find regardless of colour, including Roy 'Little Jazz' Eldridge. Like Shaw's tours with Billie Holliday, this could cause trouble especially in the Deep South, as on this tour where venues included Jacksonville, Tampa and Miami. The tour was supposed to be for a month but the final concert was cancelled ostensibly because of 'poor bookings.' According to Cecil in his report to Jed, this was untrue but the promoters had become increasingly worried about 'trouble' with the Barnet band. There had been some incidents and scuffles outside the concert venue the President Jefferson Davis Hall (A hero to the Confederate South in the Civil War) and this got worse in Tampa where the promoters were warned that if the concert went ahead that there would be 'Another Palomar,' in other words, a fire. It was signed by an organisation called the FFF (Florida for Freedom) with the signature of one Jeb Stoot (Cecil conjectured that this might be a play on the name of another Confederate hero Jeb Stuart) with an LDR counter signature. This was the second sighting of the initials LDR and Jed and Gina made a note to follow it up as well as the FFF organisation that they had not heard of until now.

Woody

It wasn't long before Cecil picked up a plum job in California; no touring, just playing and relaxing on the beach in Los Angeles and San Fransisco. 'Heaven!' he told Jed. Woody Herman had been a child prodigy on stage before taking over the Isham Jones band in 1936 and gaining the epithet 'The band that plays the blues.' This was not a great commercial idea especially in the South where on one occasion in Dallas he was told to stop playing 'those nigger blues.' Fortunately he didn't and to some his clarinet style evoked Bigard rather than Goodman, a sort of backhanded compliment. He was no reed slouch however, being chosen by Stravinsky to play his 'Ebony Concerto' at the Carnegie Hall in 1940. His band had had a 'hit' record the previous year with 'The Woodchoppers Ball' and, like his contemporaries he played all the main venues including the Glen Island Casino, the Roseland Ballroom and the 'Famous Door.'

Authors note *(The Herman Herds of Apple Honey and Four Brothers with stars such as Stan Getz, Al Cohn and Zoot Sims etc came later. The comment below about 'Nigger blues' is also true.)*

Cecil reported that he had no complaints about the band, the agent or the promoter but one incident did trouble him. This was an article in the local 'LA Messenger' following the addition of Greg Alvarez, the fiery Cuban trumpeter to the band. Apparently the paper had barely noticed Cecil in the trombone section but 'Happy' Alvarez was a different matter, a kind of Carmen Miranda on stage with a high note trumpet. No, HE could not be ignored. The article bore the title 'No Nigger Blues Here' confirming that for some in LA, this word included all non-whites as it had done for the Japanese in 1942. It went on, 'Our white bandleaders have a responsibility to us to maintain and enhance white culture and Mr Herman is a disgrace to his profession and not welcome here.'

At the end of the article a telephone number was given if people wanted to know more or to 'get involved' with turning back the tide. Once more Gina added the number to her growing pile of paper.

The Count

Peace and quiet were not to last long for Cecil when, on his last day in LA he got a call from Count Basie's agent. Was he free? Was he ever?

What a chance and what a thrill to be asked to join up with this star studded band. The downside was that it was to be a lightning tour across the USA, dubbed as the East-West Tour (A North-South tour was planned for later.) This time the venues would include Seattle in Washington State, Minneapolis in Minnesota and Chicago in Illinois. Cecil would be playing alongside Dicky Wells and Benny Morton in the three piece trombone section that 'Bill' Basie was trying out. The band was still making a name for itself after some indifferent reviews about tuning in 1937. Ironically it was in that year that they recorded what was to be one of their enduring masterpieces 'One O'Clock Jump.'and by 1938 they were becoming a force to be reckoned with. As mentioned, unlike the Brown or Barnet bands, Basie collected virtuosi in every department, Lester Young and Herschel Evans (who died in 1939) on saxes, Buck Clayton and Harry Edison on trumpets and the pulsating rhythm section of Freddie Green Walter Page and Jo Jones. Unlike the other units that Cecil had worked with recently this was primarily a 'black' band, a notable exception being Earle Warren on alto. Of course there were others around including 'The Duke' and Lionel Hampton.

Cecil's reports to Jed&Gina were full of anecdotes about the band but he did find time to reflect that, by the time they reached Chicago, there was a palpable change in the air. Blacks were out on the streets celebrating black culture in many different forms and Cecil thought it was about time. He reflected that all this might be occurring because of the perception that FDR (Roosevelt) was sympathetic to their cause having led the nation into war, not only against the Japanese but also against Hitler who he had accused of evil racism. However the jury was still out on this because he had invoked Executive Order 8802 to cancel the 'March On Washington' planned by A. Philip Randolph in 1941.

It seemed therefore that there was still work to be done, he said, but there was a sense of increased 'black consciousness' all around. Audiences were mainly Afro-American or Latino but there were a few white enthusiasts barely tolerated by the crowd. 'The biter bit' mused Jed when he got Cecil's report. Gina thought that this was rather unfair citing John Hammond the promoter who had done so much for the careers on Billie Holliday and Teddy Wilson. 'One swallow doth not a summer make' quoted Jed, 'We can't really be surprised can we?'

Follow the Money

During Cecil's tours Jed&Gina had been preparing their dossier on the STRA awards and by now they had more than a hundred. They had covered the last 4 years countrywide and had been amazed at the variety. As we know, Jed had escaped 'The Draft' but the war had dragged until 1945 only ending with the Atomic bombs at Nagasaki and Hiroshima.

By then Jed and Gina had more than 100 leads and, together with Cecil's reports they hoped to establish a list of names and organisations linked to the STRA awards. Furthermore there was just the possibility that they might find connections with other groups in the US and beyond, and even identify the charismatic leader that had eluded them so far. Above all though the thing that kept them going was the thought that the 'STRA' money trail might lead to the identification of Reuben's killers. She had decided to give herself a 'nom de phone' so as not to arouse suspicions. When she told Jed the name that she had chosen he laughed. 'Don't you think that's overdoing it a bit?' he asked. 'No,' she replied, 'trust me. I can act the part of a 'not very bright' secretary. Just wait and see.'

Miss 'Dolores Dimm'

As had been agreed it was Gina's job to telephone as many people on the list as possible. She began with a few 'blanks' but then struck lucky with 'The Memphis Tennis Club.' This is how the conversation went.

Club. 'This is Memphis Tennis Club. May I help you?'

Gina. 'Yes, thank you. I'm very sorry to bother you but I need some information and I'm hoping that you can help me.'

*　　　*　　　*　　　*

Well I'm only the telephonist here. What is it you want exactly?

I really don't want to bother you. I'm so sorry.

That's all right. Please go on I may be able to help.

Actually my name is Dolores Dimm and I'm a new employee at the STRA awards. Mr Carruthers, my boss has asked me for some information about the award made to tour club and I don't know where to start. He says it will be my fault if the papers are lost but I've only been here a few months. I think I'll get the sack if I can't give him the stuff he wants. (Here Gina choked back a 'crocodile' tear and waited)

Don't worry Miss Dimm, I'll try to help if I can. Now what do you need?

Oh please call me Dolores. You are so kind. It's just routine you know. Now just let me see, Ah yes, well firstly the date of the award. I think that it was November last year. Is that right?

I'll look it up for you. My name's Sally by the way and what a coincidence, my sister's a Dolores too. Just wait a minute.

(Gina waited for what seemed like a very long time as the phone automatically switched to Vivaldi's 'Four Seasons.' She thought that the music was 'Summer' and it seemed to her that it could be Autumn or even Winter before Sally returned. She hoped that she wouldn't have to explain the whole thing to someone else, but then Sally was back.)

'You're in luck. I've got it, and the one from two years ago.' she said.

(Gina couldn't believe her luck. Not one award but two. Now what?)

'Oh thank you Sally.' she said. 'Let's just start with last year. What was the award for, and how much was it? Do you know the bank and the cheque signatories? Mr Carruthers especially asked for those.'

Sally responded warmly commenting that her boss was just the same, always criticising and never praising. She happily gave the details. It had been for 'training,' the bank was the 'Tennessee Mutual,' the amount was $5000 and the two signatories were a Mr R Simpson (RS) and a General L. Root (LR) on behalf of H. Gina had heard of 'The Little General' as he was known, being a much—decorated General from 1918, but lately he had become a somewhat infamous author of pro-Nazi tracts. And 'Simpson' she thought, maybe some connection to the Shipping Line or just any person called Simpson?'

She felt that she was getting somewhere and now decided to ask in a rather offhand way about the previous award. She didn't want to alarm Sally so that she might call another person over. However Sally was only too keen to go on telling Gina that the award had been for the 'Strength and Happiness' programme that Gina thought sounded suspiciously like the Kraft Durch Freude 'Strength through Joy' of the Nazi minister Robert Ley. The signatories were Simpson (again) and H.P. Leggett (The senator) but most extraordinary was the amount. It was for $ 100,000 and therefore carried a third signature 'LDR for H' Sally continued, there was a copy of a 'Training programme' attached and could she read it out to her 'friend', Dolores? This seemed like an offer that Gina could not refuse and she made notes as Sally described the detail.

MEMPHIS TENNIS CLUB 'STRENGTH AND HAPPINESS'

At this club you are very privileged to be able to be the first here in the USA to benefit from a new programme of Health and Happiness that will undoubtedly lead to enhanced strength in mind and body. Members of the Club need only pay $100 and for others the fee will be $200. Most of you will be tennis players so you appreciate the benefits of fitness, but this programme is much more than that. It is the start of something wonderful and something that you will be able to share with other S&H groups across the land and overseas in due course. That is why this is not a programme for physical fitness alone, but for moral alertness in keeping with the principles of S&H that you will sign up to.

> Week One. PE, Work and Philosophy.
> Week Two. Athletics, Work and History
> Week Three Cycling Work and Economics.
> Week Four Combat, Work and Creativity.

If you carry out your assignments well you may be asked to join a more advanced group. We are always looking for young men and women who are proud of their Anglo-Saxon background and who would be prepared to fight to protect it. Please fill in the attached form and Good Luck!

*   *   *   *

When she had finished reading Sally asked, 'Is that the kind of thing you wanted to know Dolores? I don't understand it at all myself do you?'

Gina replied rather hesitantly as if she wasn't sure either, 'I don't have a clue,' she said, 'but if it keeps Mr Bossy happy then he'll stop getting on to me. I really can't thank you enough.' 'Glad I could help,' responded Sally, 'You have a good day now.' And she put the phone down. Gina sat back, feeling weak at the knees, 'Phew' she said, 'I need a drink.'

Tampa & LA

As it turned out there were quite a few positive results from a wide variety of sources, two of which deserve mention here. In Tampa, Florida it was the Masonic Hall that received $50,000 for 'Funds donated to personally thank the Lodge for their part in the election of the new Lord Mayor' and persuading him to sign up to our 'employment' programme, which stressed that employees should be of the same race as their employers, to avoid potential racial 'misunderstandings.'As Gina read this it could only mean one thing, blacks 'not welcome' here.

In Los Angeles it was Jed's turn to strike gold as he trawled through the interview documents that were piling up on Gina's desk. His eye spotted a file marked 'Office of the Chief of Police Los Angeles.' In which there were details of a cheque for $10,000 to R.S. Biere (who was the chief) citing 'dedicated and selfless service.' This did not seem extraordinary at all and Jed was about to re-file it when the date caught his eye. It was April 10th 1942 the precise date of Reuben's murder. Could this just be another coincidence or had he found Reuben's killers? He shivered as he looked at the signatories that a clerk at the Police department had revealed to Gina namely Simpson (RS), G.T Carr (GTC), Ayrshire (A), and Lisle (L) all 'On behalf of H'. (Query was H for Hamilton?) The name Simpson had cropped up many times in different forms. Maybe, he thought, others might now be using the name as a kind of front but perhaps it was that same family of the Simpson Shipping Line. The other names were new but both seemed to fit in with a Scottish connection hinted at way back when Rudolph Hess had landed there to meet with the Duke of Hamilton (he had said). Or was the rendezvous actually with the Duke of Windsor (with his wife's known liaison with Count Ciano) or even the Duke of Kent who died in that mysterious flight (also over Scotland) the following year? And there was that elusive H again.

Jed remembered Gina's table-cloth of pepper pots and fruit. Maybe she hadn't been that far out after all. The evidence was showing clues across a very wide range of persons and organisations that might be implicated, either in Reuben's murder or even that wider plot to secure white hegemony that he always suspected. And who or what was H?

Going nowhere. Getting somewhere.

Their work was done but now came the realisation that any conclusions from their research were more likely to be conjecture rather than hard evidence. Even if the money trail did seem to implicate the Chief of Police in LA (and others) they would need written evidence from other officers to make a charge stick. Maybe this could happen but Jed thought it improbable, likewise with their broader 'conspiracy' theory. They had their suspicions but little else at present. At one time it seemed that they did not stand a 'Ghost of a Chance' but then, rather unexpectedly it had been the STRA awards that had brought them close to real people and real organisations with real purpose with many indicators that such purposes were at least countrywide and most probably International.

Simply put however there was little more they could do. There would be no court cases, no trials and no guilty verdicts. Jed had acknowledged 'the facts' as he put it, but Gina wanted more. 'Isn't there anyone we could turn over our dossiers to?' she asked, 'someone or some organisation who thinks as we do? We need someone who can follow it all up, someone with clout in the right places. One day they might be able to make sense of it all. Please Jed, think, who?' Jed looked at Gina with admiration. No he wouldn't give up either. 'Do you know Gina,' he said, 'I think that you may be on to something. Do you remember way back when Cecil was telling us about Reuben's 'Gig for Zig' and the fire on the riverboat in 1932? Well you mentioned 'The Highlander Group' and I've heard recently that they're at the forefront of anti-racism at the moment. What say we share it with them? Maybe another case will crop up in the future where we might be of mutual benefit as well.'

'You're a genius,' cried Gina,' let's do it. Now!' 'Right' responded Jed, This last leg has been a bit of a 'Sentimental Journey' Don't you think, with Reuben up 'there' egging us on and Cecil just never doubting us? Come here you.' Gina did as she was bid and slipped into his arms.

'Have I told you lately that I love you?' he sang gently into her ear until she tingled all over. She didn't like to say that this was actually the very first time that he had said it, but she knew it would not be the last.

The next day they decided to make contact with the 'Highlander' group, but before they could do so Gina received a call from the FBI asking her to attend the hearings of the HUAC (see below) as a witness. This was very worrying because everyone knew of the bullying nature of McCarthy's questioning even when people had nothing to hide. She learnt that the Highlander group was under suspicion for operating as a communist 'cell' and she and Jed were not surprised when Highlander leaders decided to move their base. Contact with them was broken for quite a while and not picked up until much later.

We shall overcome.

Authors' note *This famous song become the* <u>*anthem of the Civil Rights*</u> *<u>movement.</u> It was adapted from an old gospel song and composed by Zilphia Horton the wife of Highlander director Myles Horton. We mentioned the <u>'Highlander Group'</u> in an earlier chapter. Founded in 1932 with educational and cultural aims they adapted from 1950 to be in the vanguard of the Civil Rights movement. Our story suggests a scenario in which this might have occurred.*

The post war years were dominated by a new war, a 'Cold War' in which anti communism was rife and the 'Red Scare' meant that many innocents, including actors, musicians and just about any free thinking individual could be held and interrogated by the police, and some by the HUAC (The House of Un-American Activities Committee) led by Senator McCarthy. Gina was one of these following her articles in the 'Women's Daily Press,' on 'The seeds of racism.' She said it was a frightening experience because the only question they kept coming back to was, 'Are you or have you ever been a member of the Communist Party?' Gina had not but she told Jed that she wished that she had said, 'Yes' just to see what happened. Anyway, because of this and other matters, it was some years later before Jed and Gina finally made contact with 'Highlander', and it came about in a rather unexpected fashion.

Out of the blue they received a telephone call from Reuben Junior to say that he had joined the Highlander group using their names as referees. 'I've cleaned up my act and I've been off the booze and drugs for months. That business with the Novak dame gave me quite a scare last year and now I want to do something positive with my life like Uncle Reuben in fact.' he said. (*more on Novak later*) He hoped that they didn't mind. This was a considerable surprise to them both because they had no contacts inside Highlander at that time, and the leadership there would have no reason to respect a reference from them, so why did Reuben need their help Jed asked. There seemed to be a pause on the other end of the phone as if some thinking had to be done but when the answer came it was plausible enough. 'You under estimate yourselves,' he said, 'don't forget that Gina has had a number of articles printed in the Press on social issues and you Jed, your name's always in print about the jazz scene. You've even 'pointed the finger' at nightclubs that have a segregation policy. You're both well known all right. So will you help?'

Of course they said they would, and then one day, when they were out for a walk in the Park and looking forward to a boat ride, the sound of music reached their ears with a trumpet soaring above the sound of a harmonious choir. As we know Jed was a jazz writer with his own column, 'Jazz Notes' in the New York Echo so his ears always pricked up when 'live' music of any kind was around, but on this occasion there was another reason. 'That's Reuben,' he said to Gina with the air of someone who knew what he was talking about, and she knew better than to argue. She had been there many times when he had confounded his friends with his knowledge. 'That's not Bird,' she'd heard him say, just as everyone in the room had identified Parker, 'It's early Stitt, just listen to that glissando, not Bird at all is it. Anyone care to place a bet?' Grumbling under their breath his friends would usually have to agree, it could be an expensive business otherwise.

'So what's he doing here then?' asked Gina, 'It does seem rather odd.'

'I agree but I know that sound. He's probably on tour and has picked up a lunchtime gig, probably to pay for you know what. It seems to be coming from over there. Come on.' 'Over there' seemed to be outside the Park down a muddy track crisscrossed by railway lines with signs saying, 'Trucks turning.' 'Industrial estate', 'Caution hazardous waste,' 'Railway do not cross.' 'Beware of the dogs' and a rather amusing one which simply said, 'Where there's muck there's muck.'

Gina's hopes of a tranquil boat ride were fading as Jed strode forward as if his life depended on it. 'Hurry up,' he called as she trailed some twenty yards behind with the air of a defeated prisoner of war. 'Coming' she said. Then as they turned a corner they finally saw their quarry. Outside a large factory with the name, 'South Carolina Tobacco Store,' stood a choir of maybe thirty singers, men, women and children of various races and beside them a solitary trumpet player, yes, it was Reuben for sure.

Jed now slowed up and took Gina's hand as they approached, 'Sorry about the rush,' he said, 'but I wouldn't have missed this for the world.'

Gina had to agree, as she too was entranced by the blending of voice and brass that performed that old gospel song, 'We shall overcome.'

Authors note. *A strike took place at the store in 1946. J.B. Thompson was a minister and educator and one of the leaders of Highlander.*

Perhaps half an hour went by before two men came out of the factory and the leader of the singing group went to meet them. Their discussion was brief and when it was over he turned to the choir with a very elaborate 'thumbs up' sign. As he joined their ranks amidst much backslapping they placed him on a box so that he could be clearly seen and heard.

'Brethren, Brothers and Sisters we have done it. We have finally done it. Many of you here today were with me five years ago today in 1946 when we began our campaign in support of the striking workers here. Some of our dear friends have since passed away and we thank them for their service'. He bowed his head, 'Amen.' he said and the choir responded, 'Amen.' He continued, 'The owners, the Rainiers, Walcot's and the other directors have authorised pay increases of $2 per hour with every other Saturday off. This is to be backdated and compensation paid to the families of those who have since died. What's more they have agreed to a fully racially integrated work force for the first time. You should be very proud of your achievement here today so let's finish with another song. How about 'When the Saints go marching in'? Reuben, give us that long slow start and then let's all have fun as we sing along.'

There was such a happy atmosphere that Jed and Gina just had to join in. Soon enough Reuben spotted them and gave a high 'trill' of recognition.

The music over he came across looking really pleased to see them.

'Hello you two,' he said, 'what a lovely surprise. How did you find me?'

Jed and Gina then explained that it was just a coincidence as they had heard the music from the park. 'So who are these people?' asked Gina.

Reuben smiled, 'You should know.' he said, 'This is the Highlander choir and I'm a sort of member since you sent your references, and that man over there, the important one, well that's John Beauchamp Thompson himself. Come on I'll introduce you.' They walked over to Thompson who was drinking a large glass of ginger beer with ice. 'John,' said Reuben, 'I'd like you to meet two very good friends of mine and my referees if you remember.' Thompson greeted them with a big smile, 'Yes your reputations go before you,' he said, 'I wondered about young Reuben, in fact we might have turned him down if it wasn't for your warm words. Welcome, welcome.' Jed and Gina shook the outstretched hand warmly but deep down Gina was worried. Reuben was a 'will o the wisp' she thought, just as likely to do a glorious deed and then descend into the darkness of drugs and become totally unreliable, and they, Jed and herself, seemed to be his guarantors. She rather wished that they weren't, but paradoxically that's how it came about that Jed and Gina finally met up with the 'Highlander' group.

At that first meeting they barely had time to tell Thompson their full story but he listened patiently as they told him about Reuben (Senior) and the suspicions they had about a 'racism co-ordinated' group. When they had finished he said that he had heard enough for them to submit their findings to a full committee of Highlander the very next week. 'If what you are saying is true it may be that we should be reconsidering our priorities,' he said, 'As you know our work has been mostly in the social, labour relations and educational spheres up to now but I have seen, and others have noticed that the priority of these next decades may have to be Civil Rights because if we are divided in our own house we will get nowhere on other issues that matter. A small victory here and there as you have seen today, but the big picture seems to have eluded us. I'd like you to meet our small co-ordinating committee first so that you can tell them what you have told me. Then I'd like you to address the full meeting.'

This was much more than Jed and Gina had hoped for so over the next few days they busied themselves putting together a presentation.

The first small meeting took place in a backroom at the Lutheran Church named after Danish Bishop Grundtvig who, they were told, had been such an inspiration to the group. In addition to Thompson it was attended by Mr and Mrs Horton and Septima Clark and Bernice Robinson both from the 'Citizenship Education Schools Project'.

Authors note. *Actual members of Highlander.*

There was a unanimous vote that Jed and Gina should present their findings to the larger group that afternoon giving the pair just time to have some lunch. As they sat there, there seemed to be some tension or, more precisely some anticipation and maybe a lot of trepidation as to what lay ahead. Gina played with her teaspoon and Jed just looked out of the window as if in a daze wondering what would happen next. Gina spoke first to break the ice, 'What are you going to say Jed?' she asked, 'You've convinced everyone so far, so what rabbit have you got up your sleeve this time?' He didn't seem to hear at first and just continued staring into space as if in weightlessness on a Space Mission. 'Jed' she said, 'Jed can you hear me? I asked what secret weapon you are going to surprise them with later today.' At last he moved and turned to her with a big smile. 'You,' he said, 'you are both the rabbit and the secret weapon.

You are the one they will listen to. You have passion in your voice and I've seen you tremble with emotion when you really believe in something. That's what they want to see and that's what they need to hear. I'd be far too dry, analytical even but you'll give them Fireworks.'

He was right. She was inspired. The audience laughed and they cried and then they cheered as she came to the end of her address with these words.

'Ladies and Gentlemen, Sisters and Brothers, we are at war and many of us have been asleep for decades. Our political and local leaders have successfully isolated each and every industrial, political or racial issue so that there is no cohesion on our side. But I firmly believe that they do have cohesion, organisation, and certainly commitment. Who are 'they' you ask? Well we've come a long way since we began and there are still many unanswered questions. We know that and that is why we need your help. Together we shall overcome!'

Now Thompson rose to address the crowd with these words.

'Thank you Gina. Let me say at the outset that I am very much persuaded by your argument and it could be that Highlander needs to change. Not to abandon our social conscience, indeed not, but maybe to hone it a little in these changing times. It was a little different back in Grundy in 1932 but our values remain the same. Our 'area,' if you could call it that, was the Appalachian Mountains and we had more than enough to keep us busy there. Many of our disputes then were about industrial or social disputes but now to an extent I believe that our Trade Unions do a pretty good job there, with a few exceptions of course. So what is the biggest inequality in our society today I ask you? Yes it's racism and yes maybe we should be more pro active and indeed take on a more national remit. However it won't be a 'free lunch' I can assure you. If you thought industrial relations was messy, I tell you that this will be no picnic. Now as you know Ann Braden here is already involved with the SNCC (*she was*) so I'd like you to hear her thoughts on the matter. After that we'll take a vote on the motion that we will 'take steps to expose and confront racism wherever and whenever it appears.' He sat down and Ann began.

'Sisters and brothers you probably know about some of the work that we do at the SNCC (The Student Non-violent Co-ordinating Committee) and maybe you also are acquainted with some of our leadership including Septima Clark here, but others such as the Rev. Martin Luther King, James Bevel, Bernard Lafayette, Ralph Abernathy and John Lewis are also major figures. (*they were*) We see ourselves as representing students as well as others in their struggle for basic human rights and of course we are entirely multi-racial. Increasingly though in these post war years we have found ourselves faced by two bitter enemies. Firstly, the racist KuKlaxKlan in it's many guises, including the 'American Liberty League' and others. We are accustomed to this battle; it's been going on for more than a hundred years but the other one is new. Post war USA has a new demon, the communist, or the 'Red under the Bed.' People from all walks of life are being interrogated and some imprisoned after doubtful testimony as to guilt or innocence. Many of us have been detained and we've been told, in no uncertain terms that the 'authorities' consider the Civil Rights issue to be nothing less than a communist conspiracy. It follows that they can use the long arm of the law to undertake surveillance on all of us without question. I would even suggest further, that there are many of the same people in both camps. In other words there is a 'common cause,' or a 'conspiracy' if you prefer it. I think that Jed and Gina may indeed have opened up a can of worms here and we can no longer ignore it. Let's vote.'

The vote was carried unanimously but as Highlander became more embroiled in racial matters, the 'spotlight' and the 'heat' was turned on them, being officially branded communist and forced to move.

Authors note. *It was a year later, in 1957 that the State of Georgia described the 'Highlander Folk School' as a Communist Training School, and in 1961 Tennessee revoked their licence to teach. Thompson had said that the change would be 'no picnic' and it certainly wasn't.*

This enforced change did not help Jed and Gina as information from Highlander seemed to dry up until one day they received a rather disturbing telex from Thompson. It read, 'Urgent. Get up to speed on MLK. There have been accusations about adultery and hints at a 'mole' working for the 'American Liberty League' in the SNCC or even at Highlander. Not seen Reuben lately. Have you?'

Jed turned to Gina with dismay in his voice, 'Is he saying what I think he's saying? It can't be. It just can't be. But if it is I'm responsible and it's my fault for singing his praises in that reference.' he said. As we know Gina had had her reservations for some time but she refrained from voicing them at this rather delicate point. Instead she turned to him and whispered three little words in his ear, 'I love you' she said, 'You are the nicest man I have ever known, you are straight and honest and true, and you can't believe that there are others in this world who are not the same. But they are not. No, Jedsy Lomax, you are not responsible. He is.'

But Jed was still not convinced. 'Come on Gina' he said. 'It's only a hint or more accurately an innuendo from Thompson. Let's see if there's anything more he can tell us. I'll phone him tonight and then we might be in a better position to judge whether it's likely to be him. OK?' Gina agreed and the call was made but Thompson wasn't able to add much to his telex except to say that they had been 'watching' Reuben and he could not always account for his movements. Nor could I, thought Jed, I can't always remember where I've been so that's not saying much.

He actually felt quite relieved and was about to put the phone down when Thompson added an afterthought. 'By the way,' he said. 'Not much use I suppose, but apparently the 'mole' is known as 'Ghost' on the grapevine.' Jed froze, he was speechless, he held the receiver so limply in his hand that Gina had to take it from him and place it back on the stand. She was frightened, yes Jed looked as if he had seen a ghost, but it was worse than that. 'The mole is the Ghost. It's got to be Reuben.' he said.

Authors note. '*Having concluded that MLK was dangerous due to communist influences the FBI attempted to discredit him further with accusations of extra marital affairs. Their accusations were not without some truth according to his biographer David Garrow.' (ref Wikipedia)*

It would hardly be an understatement to say that there was shock, bordering on bereavement in the Lomax household that day for when a person dies all their good and bad goes with them. Reuben had died in Jed's mind, but he was still alive and Jed could not grieve. For Gina it was slightly simpler. She had never really believed in Reuben but she was shocked just the same. Now they had another problem on their hands. The police now arrived at Jed's flat to inform him that they had an 'APB' out for Reuben regarding a 'violent affray' at the nightclub where he had been appearing as a guest with the 'Thanks for Shanks 4,' a quartet led by the virtuoso alto saxophonist Bud Shank. According to the police the fight had been over an underpayment by Reuben for a great deal of coke. The dealers wanted their money and Reuben didn't have it, 'But I can get it,' he was heard to say. Then one of the dealers smiled and said 'When?' 'Give me until tomorrow I'm meeting an important Head then.' Reuben had replied, but apparently the dealers weren't prepared to wait so it seems that Reuben took a billiard cue and smashed two of them to the ground. The police said that one of them was on life support and the incident could become one of homicide. Apparently Reuben had then left in a hurry and hadn't been seen since, and that was why they were following up possible leads from his friends. Did they know anything? Jed and Gina could honestly say that they had no idea where he might be, in fact, since the MLK incident Jed couldn't bear to think about him let alone be in touch, but he was worried just the same.

'Did you hear what the police said about where Reuben hoped to get the money from?' asked Jed. 'Yes, very strange, did he say an important hood? (gangster) or did he say he'd get the 'bread'? (money) or any name that sounds like Ted?' replied Gina with a smile, 'No I think the Police said it clearly almost slowly and deliberately as if we might give them a clue as to what it meant. They stated that Reuben had said that he was meeting an important 'Head' but search me as to what it means.'

'I don't know either,' responded Jed, 'but I think I'll search you just the same,' as, with a bound he picked her up and carried her, squealing with simulated fear into the bedroom. Later she said, 'That was nice Jed, it's been such a long time hasn't it?' She was cuddled in his arms still trembling as he stroked her hair. 'Next Wednesday week then?' he said but she was already on top of him. 'How about now?' she said.

Reuben was taken into custody shortly after, in fact he surrendered himself at Police HQ late one evening saying that his life was in danger. The police were unable to get much more out of him so, in desperation, they asked Jed and Gina to try to get him to talk. Fortunately the drug dealer had survived so the charge against him was only one of affray, and, although it took some persuasion for Jed to talk to him, they were able to post his bail and take him back to his apartment. Job done and they were just about to leave when he stopped them.

'I suppose a simple thanks won't be enough,' he said, 'and I've been thinking how I might say thank you in a more helpful way. Sure I've been playing both sides of the fence but when I need drugs, I need money. Sometimes I can manage for a short time without them but soon enough I'm hooked again and I'm sorry that I let you down again. But I can make amends, if only in a small way. You see the Police kept asking what I meant when I said that I was meeting 'an important head,' well I haven't told them. It would be more than my life's worth. I'm almost sure that the group that I work for, the ALL (The American Liberation League) has agents in the station so I've had to be careful. So here it is, just for you because if anyone finds out that I've told you, I'm a dead man. You see you've been more or less right all along. There is a group, sometimes called the 'Consortium' who seem to have agents in just about every walk of life from the legislature and judiciary right down to the Boys Brigade or the Women's Sewing Circle. Their aim is white dominance but they are patient, very patient. At present I'd say that they are building up more cells, I've heard 'him' say that for every one we lose we will create two. 'He' is the important 'Head' that I've told you about. 'He' heads up the group here in the States. I've heard him referred to as 'R' and the group as 'H' but I don't know why. My understanding is that there are eight others worldwide, now with a sophisticated communication network, but I don't know where it's based. I hope that may be some help and again, I'm sorry I let you down.'

With such penitence it was hard for Jed to resist any longer and he held out his arms and hugged Reuben like a long lost son. 'I think it will be a help in due course,' he said, 'maybe after some other pieces have fallen together. For now I suggest we all get on with life as we used to know it before we started the whole business with Uncle Reuben's death. We won't forget it but I feel that the quarry is more likely to come to us if we just do a 'soft shoe shuffle' for a while. Make your name in music Reuben. You're a great player and Gina and I are looking forward to some quality time together. The 'Consortium' will have to wait.

End Of Part Two

PART THREE
'HURRAH FOR HOLLYWOOD.'

Suicide or murder

Double Indemnity two

Reubens' story

Kenton

That Novak dame

The Informant

1954-8

The Consortium

1959-63

Miss Monroe

Consuela's story

Marilyn and me

Commitment and revelation

It was August 5th 1962 and it had been twenty years since Jed and Gina had first become fascinated by an obituary in the paper announcing the death of Reuben Solidar 'a gifted jazz musician of some note.' Their subsequent investigations with Cecil, Reuben's brother had led them layer by layer, to the conclusion that, underneath a veneer of normality, there were dark racist forces at work aiming to undermine existing norms in society and replace them with a worldwide white hegemony. They had finally passed their findings over to the 'Highlander' Group wondering if more evidence might come to light. Reuben Junior had said that he knew of a group known only as the 'Consortium' with world-wide affiliates, but with little else to go on, they felt it was a good time to have a break. That had been a few years ago, and there had been no reason to think of it again until now, as they sat and watched TV that day in August.

Suicide or murder?

Jed was slightly distracted from the TV by Gina calling from the kitchen, 'It's lamb tonight.' she said, 'Do you want white or that new rose^?' 'What? What did you say?' replied Jed, 'Sorry I wasn't listening. There's a news item just coming on about Marilyn Monroe. Better come in or you'll miss it. Oh, yes, white please.' Gina came in carrying two glasses one of white and one rose^. 'Think I'll have the rose^ instead,' laughed Jed, but Gina was having none of it. She handed him the white and snuggled next to him. 'Now' she said, 'what's this all about?' Jed put his finger to her lips to signify quiet, but she licked it just the same as they waited for a 'jingle' to finish and for the TV Announcer to continue.

'The body has been confirmed as that of <u>Miss Marilyn Monroe</u> the movie actress and further details will be available in due course. It is understood that the body was found at her home and that a young musician known to her is being questioned. Now we have some exciting news from our Sponsor. Hello Charlie what's the good news today?'

At this point the musical jingle began again, a cross between 'Follow the Yellow Brick Road' and 'Popeye the Sailor Man.' This was followed by Charlie's voice. 'Yes it's me again folks and what's Cheerful Charlie got for you today?' he began, but further information about Charlie's surprise were peremptorily cut as Jed switched the set off. 'Don't mind do you darling?' he asked, 'I can't stand that man, can you?' Gina pretended to sulk. 'Now we'll never know what it was will we?' she said and Jed laughed, 'No, but I'll give you a surprise if you don't watch out. But be serious for a minute. This could mean a whole heap of bother you know.' 'Yes it could if I missed a special offer.' Gina persisted. 'No. Not that,' replied Jed, 'Now who was it that got in touch with us last month saying he was in trouble with a famous actress even though he refused to say who?' Gina thought for a moment and then her voice sounded serious as well. 'Reuben, that's who. It was young Reuben wasn't it? I remember that he said there were 'people' out to get him, but we thought it was a touch of paranoia connected with his cocaine habit didn't we?' Jed nodded and continued, 'I think we'd better see if he's OK don't you?'

Actually they never made the call because a few moments later the phone went and it was Reuben. 'Jed,' he said, 'thank God it's you. You've got to get me out of this. They've stitched me up with the Monroe affair. They say they'll probably charge me with murder. Murder! I wasn't anywhere near her place. I'm innocent but the cops just want me to confess and I can't because I didn't do it. Jed, you've got to help me or I'm done for. Dad always said you were the best investigative reporter around and I can't trust anyone else. No-one, nobody, do you understand?' Jed thought for a moment and then said. 'The best thing you can do Reuben is to keep calm. We've just heard it on the news but give us a few days and we'll fly over to see you.

The State will provide a lawyer at first and then we can see about bail. OK?' 'Please hurry, I heard them talking about that Novak case, way back, as if there was some connection. You've got to get me out of here fast.' 'I will,' said Jed, 'but you must promise to tell me nothing but the truth. Do you understand?'

'Sure. I promise,' replied Reuben, 'I've got nothing to hide, Nothing.'

'So, did you know Marilyn Monroe and if so, when did you meet?' he asked. 'Yes I'd met her a couple of times usually after a concert. First time was sometime last year when I did that concert with Goodman. She was there with Luciano.' 'Fine,' said Jed, 'that's a start. Hang on in there and we'll be in touch soon. Me and Gina, that is.' The phone went dead maybe out of allowed police cell time, and Jed looked at Gina with a resigned shrug of the shoulders. 'Looks like we're hooked again.' he said.

Gina stared at him with that same forlorn look and just said, 'Hooked maybe, but on a line with an alcoholic druggie and general dropout. You realise we won't be able to believe a word he says don't you?' 'Yes I do, I sure do,' replied Jed, 'but we've got to help haven't we, if not for his then surely for the sake of his uncle and his dad of course. They won't let him out for at least a week and that gives us some time doesn't it? Now, don't laugh but I'd like to make a suggestion. Because we know that he'll lie to us I suggest that we use the time that we have in gathering as much information about Miss Monroe to see if it ties up with what he says, You know dates, places, mutual friends etc.' Gina thought hard for a moment and, when she spoke she seemed somehow animated and excited as if she'd had a brainwave that would help to solve the case

That's a great idea Jed,' she began, 'but I'd like to take it further. Just hear me out. He mentioned that Novak affair back in '54 so there may be some similarities there so what I suggest is this. Now don't laugh but I suggest that we take one case each, find out what we can and then present it, as a kind of play, to the other. In that kind of dramatic setting we might just open up a few avenues that could remain hidden with a more normal and straightforward fact finding exercise.' Jed looked somewhat bemused, 'I don't see how making it up would help,' he said, 'we'll have enough trouble getting the real facts as it is.' However there was no stopping Gina, 'That's the whole point Jed. It's because we won't have all the facts that a dramatic recreation might help. You know, to fill in the gaps; and if our hunches turn out to be wrong, well and good but there's a chance we might hit on something. Anyway we can't do anything else for a few days and we're bound to find out something and it'll be fun. I've decided, I'll take the Novak case and you take Monroe. OK?' Jed knew when he was beat, 'Right Miss Marple, race you to the library.' he said.

For the next few days they both busied themselves with research into the 1954 and 1963 cases, Gina the former, and Jed the latter. They both wanted to know why a young black musician had been linked with two famous white actresses if it wasn't true. Maybe that part of the story was true, but as to sexual harassment and now murder, well that all sounded rather unbelievable so what could be behind it?

Gina found out soon enough that another figure appeared in the Novak story about this time and that was Sammy Davis Jnr, he of the Dean Martin, Frank Sinatra Rat pack. Actually this 'affair' had been kept quiet for some time until 'Confidential,' (a gossip magazine) ran an expose^. This placed her career in peril in some quarters but did little to harm Davis' reputation as a bad boy; probably the opposite. So Novak's agent and the various interests in her 'budding' career at this time would not have taken kindly to another inter-racial idyll and might well have intervened to make any news that did leak out a matter of assault rather than consensual sex. Ms Novak denied even knowing young Reuben but she had reported a burglary that the police were investigating.

(Author's note. *Kim was 20 in 1954 and had just had a bit part in a film 'The French Line.' It was Columbia who changed her name from Marilyn (coincidentally). That year she also starred in 'Pushover' and then played the 'femme fatale' role in 'Phffft' opposite Jack Lemmon. She dated Sammy Davis Jnr in the 1950's and went on to star in Picnic (1955) and Hitchcock's Vertigo (1958).)*

Meanwhile Jed was digging into the far more recent Monroe affair. This case tended to be a much more explosive one because of her alleged relationships with the Mafia boss Sam Giancarna and one if not more, members of the Kennedy Clan. What's more she was dead. Reuben had been picked up by the police following a 'tip off' and it was this last item that interested Jed, namely who provided the 'tip' and why?

(Author's note. *Marilyn was 37 in 1963 and unlike Kim, it seemed that she was reaching the end of her career. She had stormed onto the scene back in 1952 with 'Niagara' and followed this up with 'Gentlemen Prefer Blondes' the following year, stopping off to pose for Playboy. She was THE Sex symbol of the age (Some like it Hot 1959) but struggled to find critical acclaim as an actress. This did come with 'Bus Stop' (56),'The Prince and the Showgirl' (57) and 'The Misfits' in 1960 with Clark Gable. Her brief marriage to Arthur Miller revealed a serious side to an otherwise somewhat frivolous reputation most publicly demonstrated in her Birthday tribute to JFK in 'that' dress. Her friendship with Sam Giancarna was well known and rumours persisted of affairs at 'Lilliput.' By 1962 she was in free fall, or maybe just falling as 20th Century Fox had to renegotiate her contract due in part to unreliability issues. Somewhat ironically as far as our story goes, she had been replaced by* <u>Kim Novak</u> *in the film 'Kiss me Stupid' co-starring Dean Martin.)*

Double Indemnity Two

The next morning Gina was ready to present her 'Novak' story. Whilst she had been in the planning stage, she kept thinking of the film 'Double Indemnity' and decided to present it to Jed along those lines. She began by setting the scene. 'Scene One, an Insurance office' she said.

Scene one.
The Malibu Insurance Offices

Seated at his desk in shirtsleeves sat a rather harassed looking man poring over a case file that was on his desk. The name his door was Edward G. Robinson Head of Claims, and it was he who would narrate the story. He had just come upon a case that made him feel uneasy. He picked up his Dictaphone and began to speak into it to record his observations.

Authors' note. *As stated Kim's name was linked with Sammy Davis Jnr.*

'The word on the street was that a promising blonde actress was playing away from home with a Black Tom (excuse my French), a musician or actor they said he was, but anyway he'd been picked up in no time on a charge of aggravated assault and burglary from her flat. Sure she'd made an insurance claim for some missing items, some furs and jewellery but nowhere had she mentioned an assault. In fact she hadn't mentioned anyone she suspected of the crime so why had the police picked him up? Name of Solidar, one of Kenton's band, good too I've heard but I didn't like the sound of it. Why? Because the little man in my stomach told me that it was all too pat. What was she up to, this dame I thought, and what were the police doing making a meal of it? I decided that the best thing to do was to send my best man around to see her, put some meat on the potatoes; find out what sounded legit. He had a good nose for that sort of thing and I'd have trusted him with my life. His name was Jed Lomax.'

(Here Gina giggled as she turned to Jed. 'Artistic licence, now you're a movie star.' she said, 'Hero or villain I wonder?'

'He said he'd go down to interview the Novak broad and give me the low down the next day but I was in for a shock. Sure he came into the office but he was looking uncomfortable. He was usually a calm guy, now he was sweating. The little man in my stomach started to play up. What's going on I wondered. 'OK Jed let's hear it.' I said and waited for him to begin. His hands glistened with sweat and there were beads on his brow.

'Hot day,' I said and moved to open a window, 'Is that better?' 'Yes thanks,' he replied but he was still sweating.

(Gina was enjoying this. 'Cut to the Novak apartment' she said.)

Scene Two.
The Novak Apartment Beverly Hills

A man was at the door in a trilby hat and a long raincoat but it wasn't raining. She opened the door and looked him up and down.

'I phoned' he said, 'Name's Lomax.'

'Yes,' she replied, 'Come on in.'

She walked before him, swaying her hips as she approached a very large settee. She then sat down and crossed her legs in a languid fashion.

'Smoke?' she said, handing him a Dunhill and a Gold lighter.

'Sure' he replied lighting hers first. She steadied the flame with her hand as if it was a two-man job and a moment too precious to be hurried.

'Mmm nice' he said 'Gold and initialled. Present?'

'Would you like to give me a big present?' she asked provocatively.

'Cut the crap,' he said, 'Tell me about Solidar.'

'Nothing to tell,' she replied, 'never heard of him.'

There followed a silence that you could have cut with a chainsaw.

'So?' she said.

'Is it so?' he replied.

'Is what so?' she responded.

'You know,' he said, 'Solidar.'

'What do you think?' she murmured softly.

'You tell me.' he said.

'Can't you guess?'

'In that case, yes.'

'Or no.' she whispered.

'If you say so.'

'Do I?

'Look this is getting nowhere.'

'Do you want to get somewhere?' she asked.

Now she moved imperceptibly closer to him on that large and very comfortable settee. He quickly stood up and backed away. 'I can see that I'm wasting your time and you mine. I'm sorry to have troubled you.'

'Well actually I'm not troubled at all,' she said, 'but I can see that you are. You're sweating. You wish you knew whom I'd been to bed with. You wish you knew what it was like and you wish it was you. Right?'

By now Jed was at the door but turned as he opened it. 'Right.' he said.

(Gina looked at Jed and said, 'Now we're back in the Insurance Office.')

Scene Three.
The Malibu Insurance Offices. (Robinson continues his story)

I could see that something was troubling Lomax but I didn't let on. The little man in my stomach was playing up again and, when that happens I've found it's better to smoke out trouble rather than to set a fire. I decided to wait and see what turned up after I sent him to quiz Solidar. This wasn't going to turn out well I told myself but could I have been wrong? The next day he came in as bright as a button and sat down.

'There, I knew it' he said, 'The police are sure it's him. Seems he was there after all. He'd left some of his stuff behind, probably as he was rummaging for valuables. Case closed. What's next?' Now, as I said before, I'm a rather cautious guy when it comes to drawing quick conclusions, so I just told him he'd done a good job and put him onto a car claim that might take up some time while I figured out what to do.

I still felt that something was wrong so I decided to case her joint to see if my suspicions were true, and they were.

('Another scene change' said Gina. 'Now we're outside her apartment.')

Scene Four
Outside Miss Novak's apartment. (Robinson continues)

I switched the engine off a few yards from the house and cruised up under a large tree. It was drizzling and the screen was steaming up so I opened the windows and got rain over my new coat. Someone's going to pay I thought, but just then there was the sound of another motor-car and I ducked down and peered over the steering wheel. I didn't want to see what I saw but I knew it would be him. Yes, it was Jed all right. The lights stayed on for a while and I saw two figures, some feet away from each other as if they were talking. Nothing else seemed to happen for a time then, just as I blinked, the two shapes became one and disappeared from my view. Soon after the lights went out and I was left, cold and damp, wondering whether to see if anything else happened. I finally decided that I'd seen enough and headed for home and a hot bath.

I couldn't be sure what to make of this new development so I went to see Sergeant Murphy at Police HQ the next day.

Scene Five
Police HQ

Murphy greeted me in his broad Irish brogue. 'Sure if it isn't the man with a bee in his bonnet.' he said, referring to my general persistence and unwillingness to take anything for granted. 'I know why you're here. It's bound to be about the Novak 'Colleen' isn't it? Well you're wasting your time I can tell you. It's him for sure it is. He's the guy, Solidar, no doubt about it. He was there and here's the evidence picked up in her flat. See, it's his watch, gold with his initials RS embossed in silver.' I took the watch from his hand and looked at it carefully then returned it to him with a smile. 'Is that all you have/' I asked. 'Well, what more do you want,' he replied, 'a photograph of him in the flat?' I couldn't help smiling because I quite liked Murphy, although to be honest he wasn't the brightest of cops. 'Have you ever heard of Rudolf Suisse, the Swiss clockmakers?' I asked innocently. 'Can't say I have,' Murphy replied, 'but what's that got to do with it?' I didn't know how to put it without hurting his feelings but it had to be done. 'RS and the shape of the logo in 'German' or 'Teutonic' script shows this watch to be a Rudolph Suisse for sure. It probably never belonged to Solidar and it's very doubtful that he could have afforded such an expensive item, probably $5000 or more. Sorry.'

Murphy looked somewhat crestfallen but soon recovered. 'I suppose I should say thanks,' he said, 'despite what you may think we don't like to lock up innocent men.' 'Yes, you'll have to let him go,' I said, 'but tell me, who was it that 'fingered' him for the job?' At this point Murphy began to look nervous and evasive, 'Sure Edward,' he said, 'let's not go there. I'll drop charges, let's leave it at that.' Edward or not, Murphy hadn't accounted for that little man in my stomach who just wouldn't let go. 'You'll have to tell me Patrick,' I said, also adopting the familiar but now in a somewhat threatening tone. 'It's me or a Grand Jury.' 'Have it your way,' he said, 'actually it was that guy from Columbia studios, you know, Frank Pacelli, said they knew something and I should check it out, to protect Miss Novak you see.' I said thanks and left. It was all beginning to make sense. Columbia had only recently avoided a scandal with Novak and Sammy Davis and they didn't want another one. What better way to kill two birds with one stone than to frame Solidar for burglary and throw in sexual harassment for good measure? I decided to look up the Columbia directors and stockholders to see who called the shots. They were Goldman Sachs, General Motors, Nabisco and the Simpson Shipping Line. The names didn't mean much to me but strange as it may seem, my stomach settled down soon after.

Jed and I parted company soon after and I found out later that he was an agent for McCarthy and the HUAC. My stomach never let me down.'

(Author's note. *The House Committee on Un-American activities took the Red Scare of the 1950's very seriously indeed. Many Hollywood stars were interrogated and some banned. This was also a time when Black Civil rights activities were becoming prominent, and many tended to conflate these two as identical threats, stating that Commies and N . . . . are the same and neither can be trusted.*)

'That's it.' announced Gina, 'End of play. What do you think?' Jed clapped loudly as if in a theatre. 'Bravo Gina, what a story.' he said, 'maybe, just maybe you could be onto something. Well done. Now come here and make as if you're Kim and I'm the 'other' Jed Lomax.'

The next day Jed was supposed to take his turn and present the 'Monroe' case to Gina, but a desperate call from Reuben persuaded them to go and see him immediately. They had posted his bail and also paid for a room for him at the same hotel that they had booked into. Now they waited to hear his account of events past and present with much scepticism.

Reuben (Junior's) Story

Unlike his father and uncle, young Reuben had soon become dependent on alcohol and drugs in his life as a musician, and he freely admitted that he would obtain money from anywhere to feed his habit. Much to Jed&Gina's surprise he told them, without a hint of guilt, that he had been a paid informant to a group that he only knew as 'All America.'

'They paid well,' he said, 'What do I care about their angle?' Jed was quite offended by this admission but kept quiet for now preferring to take things a step at a time. He began, 'Tell us Reuben, what happened to you after that Novak affair back in 54?' Reuben hesitated as if uncertain and then said, 'Nothing really. I was under suspicion for a time but when they couldn't find evidence they had to let me go and soon enough I got a job in the movies myself.' Gina spoke up now, 'I don't think we know much about that part of your life,' she said. 'Why don't you tell us, because it does seem as if there may be connections in the movies doesn't it?' Once more Reuben looked rather nonplussed so Jed spelt it out, smiling at Gina as he did so, after all this part of it had been her idea in her play.

'It's possible that you wouldn't know much about it,' he said, 'but at the time of the 'Novak' affair there was a great deal in the press about 'Reds under the Beds,' you know, the Communist scare, and the Civil Rights movement was also seen to be threatening. Many movie stars were interviewed by the HUAC and some banned. Others may have been 'persuaded' to back off from demos and the like by violence to them or their families. What we're saying is that you might have just been a convenient scapegoat in both cases but if so we'd like to know who would have organised it and why'. 'This is all above my head,' protested Reuben, 'I need a drink.' 'Let's not forget that you're out on bail on a serious charge,' interjected Jed, 'OK let's all have a drink but only if you begin at the beginning and take us through those 'Novak' years.' It was done, the compromise made, Reuben got his booze and they got his story.

He began, 'As you know I was with the Kenton band at the time . . . .

Kenton and the West Coast scene

As you know I was with the Kenton band at the time. What arrangements, what musicians, what power, what soloists! Formidable! (French pronun.)

At one time or another he had reedmen Lee Konitz, Art Pepper, Stan Getz or Jimmy Giuffre, trombones Milt Bernhardt or Frank Rosolino with Shorty Rogers on trumpet, Stan Levey piano and Shelley Manne drums.

I'd actually joined part time in 1950 just as the band was coming to the end of a long experimental era that had really started way back in the 40's. At that time Stan had begun to create a unique sound in what was then a fairly predictable world of Big Band Swing. His 'Artistry in Rhythm' was an early example and, when Pete Rugulo joined as arranger, the band became increasingly 'avant garde,' sometimes emulating impressionist European composers such as Ravel. 'Intermission Riff was a prime arrangement whilst 'Peanut Vendor' became a world-wide hit and I was in the 12 piece trumpet section. After recording sessions or concerts some of the guys used to drift around in nightclubs for jam sessions and eventually Shorty put a different, somewhat smaller band together. He called it the Giants and it became kind of synonymous with what became known as the 'West Coast' scene easily identified by the addition of Johnny Graas on French horn. It could still amount to a 17 piece and sometimes I got to sit in. I think that that's when I met Suzy but I can't remember much about it, because I was generally high on a cocktail of drugs and alcohol, but then, so was everyone else.

Some of us on the LA scene got a big break a few years later in 1954 when they decided to make the 'Glenn Miller Story' with Jimmy Stewart and June Allyson. I saw it as a good opportunity to get my hands on some serious 'coke.' and I managed the musical scores just fine. I don't suppose I need to tell you this but of course I didn't appear in the film because all of the AEF musicians were white in wartime, and all regiments were segregated as well. I suppose I was following in Uncle Reuben's footsteps when he had played as 'Ghost' musician on some very important recordings way back. I know for a fact that it was his solo on Chu Berry's 'Ghost of Chance' but they wouldn't admit to it, in public anyway. I felt quite good about doing the same thing. Anyway the film wasn't a whitewash, forgive the pun, because Louis made a guest appearance. Never know with Satchmo do you? Was he an Uncle Tom or just a great, maybe the greatest jazzman ever, probably a bit of both.

Author's note, *President Truman desegregated the Forces after the war.*

At this time I spent a lot of time with Paul Dugard because we were the only two blacks on the set and he seemed to have easy access to the 'dope' that I had begun to crave for so badly. The trouble was that he had other interests too, namely the 'pretty white dolls' in Miss Allyson's entourage, and this could be dynamite if it got out, and of course it did. Paul usually did well with the girls. He came from New Orleans and was really a Creole like many from that city so I suppose he could pass as white (ish) in some situations especially if it was a gloomy nightclub which it often was when the girls came out to 'play.' We both got called 'Whitey' for the way that we seemed to fit in with the white crowd. Anyway he met up with a young blonde called Delphine, from Oklahoma, pretty as a picture and innocent as they come. Well she was for a while if you know what I mean so soon enough Paul got his marching orders. There was plenty of flirting on the 'Set' but black on white was a different matter entirely. Apparently the management board told him that they had been 'leaned on' by the powers that be' who would not countenance any racial scandal.

He said that I should get the sack as well for being too close to some other movie stars of the time, I think he had Kim in mind, but fortunately she wasn't working for the same studio so it remained kind of secret until the day that I was picked up. That was a shock let me tell you and this is how it came about. That Novak dame was extraordinary . . . .

'That Novak Dame', Reuben's Story.

That Novak dame was extraordinary you know. From the first time I saw her I knew that she was trouble, just too lovely and only 20 at the time. There were bees swarming all the way from San Diego to Santa Cruz and she was the Honey. That night at Quaglino's I was onstage with a group led by John Lewis (later of MJQ fame) when I noticed her looking at me. At least I thought she was but couldn't be sure so I avoided eye contact and carried on playing but mind elsewhere. 'What you doin' man,' called out John from the piano, 'that's an Ab not a Gdim, where you goin' man?' I nodded in his direction and finished off my solo rather hurriedly. Fortunately it was the interval so I made my way to the bar. John and the others came up but instead of criticising they were all smiles. 'I think he in love.' said Percy (Heath) the bass player, 'Sure nuff,' said John, 'he sure is,' and with that they walked away laughing to the dressing room and I was left alone. But only for a moment because I became aware of the smell of perfume behind me that made my hair stand on end, and I knew it was her. I turned and she smiled, 'Hello Reuben,' she said, 'would you mind lighting my cigarette As you can see I've only got one hand free?' 'Sure' I muttered feeling quite tongue-tied as she handed me a gold embossed lighter. 'Thanks,' she whispered as she took my hand and guided it close to her shining lips, then blew a smoke ring straight back in my face with a smile.' 'Trick I learnt,' she said, 'I bet you know a few tricks. How would you like to come to a party later? Here's the address.' She handed me a folded piece of paper and then she was gone, disappearing in to the crowd with a sway of her hips. I suddenly realised that I still had her lighter and went to call after her but she'd vanished, give it to her later I thought, good excuse to go to the party anyway. I couldn't finish the last set quick enough and funnily enough I blew up a storm as if to say, 'there you are folks, listen good, this is Reuben Solidar, remember the name.' I said my goodnights and left by the back door making my way to the address that she had given me. I knew the street but not the apartment until I got near and then I realised it belonged to Sammy Davis Junior, him of the 'Rat Pack,' and quite a few of them were there, Dean Martin, Sinatra and Jerry Lewis plus some other 'cool' musicians from the scene including Chet Baker. He was always around if there was a sniff of marijuana or cocaine. Other stars and especially aspiring starlets appeared from time to time including Marilyn who was filming 'The Seven year Itch'. That's the film that had the billowing dress over the grating and I can tell you it caused quite a stir. Doris Day had 'made it' in the movies by then after her stint as vocalist with Les Brown back in the 1940's and she made rare visits to these parties. I suppose she was that little bit older but still lovely and she remained very popular with musicians who recognised her star quality. In 1954 she was in the Warner Bros 'By the Light of the Silvery Moon' a comedy with Gordon McRae.

And so it began. I don't know why but Kim kinda liked me and she opened the door to some really fancy places and people. I often saw Sammy there. That was one of those open secrets you know. 'Just Friends' as the song goes but most people thought different, and it would have remained so if it wasn't for an 'expose^' article by 'Confidential,' that Hollywood scandal rag that everyone hated but read just the same. But as I was saying, she was very good to me and introduced me to some very fine folk including many members of European aristocracy. There were Russian princes and Austrian Duchesses, minor royalties and families such as the Rainiers from Monaco and even the Duke of Windsor was there sometimes with his wife. They were an odd couple. More often than not they came as a threesome with her ex husband in tow. Frequently the Duke seemed left out as if grateful for crumbs from her table.

As I've told you I was often quite high on drugs but I did notice that Simpson and the Duke never spoke to me, unless it was to ask me to bring a drink, 'Hey you boy, three G&T's over here. Make it snappy.'

Kim made up for it though. Sometimes, when they had all gone she'd snuggle up to me and say, 'I wish there were more like you Reuben. Everywhere else I look there's always complications, with Sammy and the Studios and especially with Wallis (Simpson) and her entourage. Actually it seems more like a 'cabal' at times with all their plotting. I overheard them say once that they were in touch with the 'Fuehrer', well there's only one of those isn't there and I thought that he was dead.'

She sighed as if it was all too much for her and snuggled even closer.

While all this was going on I as playing quite a bit with different bands, usually quartets of one sort or another. I did a stint with Chico Hamilton at Bird's Bar in Central Avenue LA. This had become the West Coast's 52nd Street since Bird played there. Chico was a fine drummer, and he was another one of those looking for that 'special' unique sound that would mark him out. He found it eventually but I wasn't part of the plan. His group turned to another form of chamber music, not unlike the MJQ but with different instrumentation. He had Buddy Collette on flute and tenor and Jim Hall on guitar with the addition of a cello. (Fred Katz). Most of these 'muso's' were not involved in the politics of the day, with Martin Luther King and his bunch of radicals but sometimes we knew that doors were being shut. Often it was the agents just doing the bidding of the promoters who usually explained it in terms of the 'shareholders'. To be truthful one never knew and, to an extent the tide was turning in our favour but I didn't care as long as I got enough money for dope. That group I told you about 'All America' they paid well and it wasn't my fault if someone I 'mentioned' to them ended up with a broken nose. No, not so long as I got my dope. Funny though there were still many who suspected me of acting as a double agent, you know, giving the low down on 'All America' to the NAACP' probably because it was well known that Uncle Reuben had been involved with them. Maybe I was just too naïve to think that I'd get involved and that's why I was so shocked when I was picked up by the police for burglary and assault.

The police said that Kim had accused me but I didn't believe that for a moment. True I'd never 'made it' with her and she might have wondered why. Well, there was Suzy of course but I kept that a closely guarded secret as well. No there was something, someone else in the picture I'm sure. She had had a few new visitors recently but I hadn't paid much mind to it until now. There was one in particular I remember, tall man, always wore a hat, even in the apartment. I felt sure that I'd seen him with the Simpson crowd and those political guys who were often buzzing around. I also remember that Kim had told me to 'be careful' once after he'd paid a visit but I didn't know why and neither did she. Strange though, shortly after that I got a firecracker through my front door and a brick through the window with a note, 'Black Commie

Bum.' it said. Anyways they held me for a few days on 'clear evidence' according to them, then just as suddenly I was released with no explanation. I suppose I could have tried to find out why it all happened but I was happy enough just to go back to playing and my 'sidelines.' The downside was that Kim cut me dead afterwards saying that she couldn't be seen with me.

'It could mean a real problem for me, and probably curtains for you.' she said. I didn't like the sound of that at all and after all there was still Suzy.

The Informant.

I said that I carried on with my sidelines and that meant feeding information to the 'All America' group. I'm not proud of myself but that's just the way it was. You'd understand if you ever met someone on dope. He'd do anything even murder to get a fix. There are so many drug related tragedies in the Jazz world, Billie was one of the first and then there was Bird of course. That recording of 'Loverman' was made when he could hardly stand but it's beauty lies in that very vulnerability and starkness. Soon after they carted him off to Camarillo for rehab and he paid tribute to it later with his recording of 'Relaxing at Camarillo.'

Now take Art Pepper, so fluent with Kenton and his own groups in tunes like 'Suzy the Poodle' with Russ Freeman (did he mean 'my' Suzy?) no, I don't think so, then, when drugs took a grip it was a different story, 'Over the Rainbow' is a prime example, tortured you might say. I don't suppose I knew or cared much if I hurt others, the $ for dope was all that mattered and there were plenty out there to take advantage.

In my case it was a guy called Bill Black. He laughed when he introduced himself, told me not to take it too literally but that he was on the side of the 'Angels' as he put it, those who were trying to combat segregation but that they were hamstrung because they couldn't get information and that is where I would come in, and I would be paid very well. So, what did I think? It seemed like a no-brainer, money for old rope or more precisely money for old dope. When he could see that I was hesitating he pressed a wad of $10 bills in my hand. 'Think about it.' he said and walked off. When I looked later there were fifty of them, $500 and I was hooked. It was only later that I found out what it was that they wanted to know, personal things, contractual things, rumours, scandals and the like, anything that might besmirch a man's character, for they were only after men and only black men at that. Still, as you know and as I said I went along with it for the cash. When I found out that a black senator had committed suicide because of some revelations about his private life (witnessed at first hand by me and reported to Bill), I hardly felt any remorse. It was his survival or mine in my book and I've always been a survivor, at least I was until now.

*　　*　　*　　*

At this point Jed and Gina decided that it was best to have a break to discuss any implications that Reuben's account of the 'Novak' affair might bring to the more current issue, namely his arrest over the Monroe death. They travelled back in silence to their hotel both too pre-occupied to say a word and when they arrived Jed headed immediately for the drinks counter, hastily pouring two stiff Bourbons and calling out, 'Gina, scotch on the rocks, come and get it.' There was no reply but the bathroom door was open, so she wasn't in there. Next he looked in the bedroom and yes there she was, fast asleep with hair all tousled under the pillow. 'A double for you then Jed me lad.' he said and downed them both in single gulps. Soon he was asleep beside her and there was no stirring (of any kind) until the morning when they slipped into a warm embrace to welcome the dawn. Jed ordered breakfast for the room and with that over Gina sat cross-legged on the bed. 'So, what do you think?' she said, 'was I right or was I right?' Jed laughed, 'I must admit, your play had some very strange coincidences with his story and in a way I think that makes his story more believable. Remember our main concern was that he would lie through his back teeth. I think it's pretty obvious that there were those out to frame him but who and why are still a mystery aren't they?' Gina thought for a moment before she replied, as if 'her' story was the true account. 'Not such a mystery Jed, just a few options I think you'll agree.' 'Yes in fact I do, he replied, 'and the same names seem to be coming up don't they? Now let's get back to Reuben before they lock him up and throw away the key. I want to hear what he's got to say about those missing years from 1954. Ready? Let's go.'

Those missing years 1954-58

(Reuben continues his story)

I can't remember much about those years. Eventually the drugs caught up with me and I jumped off a bridge after a gig, trumpet and all. Fortunately they fished me out and I was sent to a clinic to dry out. Those weeks were torture I can tell you but it seemed to work for a time. The clinic was called 'Grasslands' and shortly after I came out I wrote the song. It got to be a big hit with Bob Dylan and I was back on the scene again with a real peach. It was to be a role in a film called 'I want to live' featuring the Gerry Mulligan Quartet with Art Farmer instead of the unreliable Chet Baker. Susan Hayward took the lead role. Sidney Poitier was supposed to be in the film also but was prevented due to contracts. Nowadays the film, and especially the jazz score by Johnny Mandel is considered to be a classic and the west coast musicians who took part were of the highest quality including Bill Holman, Pete Jolly and Shelley Manne amongst others. It's strange how I got the job because it was rather like racial prejudice in reverse but I didn't care. Just being close to Art Farmer and the other guys was magical. I was to be in the Orchestra that played the mood music behind the scenes and, probably because they were short of actors, I got a bit part as an extra. I was to be a down and out musician on drugs. Talk about type casting! This is how it came about. You probably know the old joke 'Somewhere there's music how high the Mafia' (moon) well that's how it was. If it wasn't one Capo and family it was another, with fingers in every pie, from bookings, catering and transport to the musicians, gigs concerts and recordings. The big name in the music business in LA at this time was 'Pro Gambino' so called because, from a very young age his ruthless streak had been observed by a rival gang. 'Not ruthless,' said his 'Capo' at the time, 'just professional. If I want something done I'll ask Gambino. He does a professional job. The name stuck and he became 'Pro' Gambino. In a big project like a film, he always had to work with others to deliver the whole package or show and sometimes there could be friction. Who came out on top could be a matter of gentle persuasion or sometimes coaxing of a more extreme kind.

In the case of the film that we were starting on 'I want to live' there was already some trouble between the Sidney Lumet producers and the financial backers who were a consortium of some sort. These backers had tried to insist on an all white cast and had managed to sideline Sidney Poitier already. It seemed that the catering and booking had been arranged on the same basis, but that transport remained a sticking point. In fact it was the Unions who insisted on a multi racial group of drivers etc and, as you know the power behind many unions was the Mafia.

It looked like stalemate and no film, until one of Gambino's gang approached me with a compromise deal. Gerry had insisted on Art Farmer but the rest of the musicians were white so would I agree to opt out of the music and just play the 'bit part' which wasn't to be a musician either, but a fool of a waiter. I'd be well paid of course. Well, as I said before where is pride when you need a fix? However I'm not dim and I could see that they needed this white veneer in the film so that the transport could be agreed, quietly and behind the scenes, to be multi racial. Yes, I'm not dim so I asked for double his suggested price, and I got it. If I'd given it more thought I think I'd have wondered what it was all about and why having a white cast film (apart from token blacks) could be so important. However I've begun to realise that perception is often more important than fact, and the idea that America is white squeaky clean was the one that was being promoted. Not only that, but that one of the bastions of Negro culture was being emaciated. In a film where musical artistry was the key there could be no Afro-America, yes there had been 'jazzers' in the past but these were naïve, folksy performers. The subtext was that 'Jazz Art is White.' Funny though, the trumpeter was 'Black and Art,' (Farmer) and that seemed to contradict their whole premise; but as I said I didn't give it much thought.

At this point Gina interjected with a question. 'I've noticed Reuben,' she said, 'that this 'Consortium' as you call it, keeps cropping up. In many ways they seem to be the power brokers behind the scenes, would you agree, and if so do you know anything more about them?'

Reuben thought for a moment and then smiled, 'Not much I suppose but I did find out something purely by accident and I'll tell you about it.'

The Consortium & the Covenant

'You're right' Reuben continued, 'I have come across some of the same guys from time to time and it's not always in the same situation. One time it's about bookings and another time catering for example, but it's the same faces all right. Now you'd think it was the Mafia wouldn't you, but they TAKE your money, this crowd GIVE you money and plenty of it if they get their way. I've found out that they are also very generous with small business and, provided that everyone signs the 'Covenant' they get the dough. Yes, that's what they call the agreement that they ask for and it's very, very secret. Paul Johnson who actually was a NAACP agent (as well as a fine trombonist) ended up on the slab, 'murder unsolved,' because they found out he was digging around. However, I did find out something by chance as I said before, but I've kept it secret until now.

Suzy and me used to take time out in an old Winnebago camper van parked in a lot behind the studios. It could get very hot in there if you know what I mean but it was out of the way and usually there was no one around at night. On that particular night we both heard a kind of rumbling sound as we were stretched out on the convertible bed. 'What's that?' I said, pricking up my ears. 'Nothing Rubie,' Suzy whispered, 'it's nothing, probably a late delivery or something.' 'No,' I said,' sounds more like a car. Could be a robbery, I think I'll take a look.' Suzy laughed, 'I suppose you're going to take on an armed gang in THAT condition, are you?' I grinned, 'Give me a minute,' I said, 'and those 'hoodlums' (I used movie talk), won't know what's hit them.' Saying which I crept to the window and gently pulled back the curtains. I wasn't really prepared for what I saw. There wasn't one car but two. No three. No four. No five, they were coming in fast and there was a uniformed man at the gate guiding them into the inner courtyard of the studio. I called over to Suzy, 'Come and look, what do you think this is all about?' I said, 'Search me,' came the reply, 'in fact that's a good idea, come over here and search me. I surrender.' Suzy never could take things serious so I just waved a hand behind my back, 'In a mo.' I said, 'just let me watch this for a minute.' I could see through the gate that the cars,(a better description would be Limos, because they were all black Cadillacs), had stopped and chauffeurs were opening doors for men in suits. I noticed one in particular, tall, greying hair and distinguished. But what I noticed more was that the left arm of his jacket was folded across his chest. I concluded that he only had one arm but what was even more extraordinary, and I couldn't be sure because it was dark, he seemed to have a patch over his right eye. I should have been thinking 'spooky' but I wasn't.

I was thinking Stauffenberg, Hitler's would be assassin. He was a mirror image but I knew that it couldn't be because he had been executed back in Berlin after the plot had failed. Furthermore if I saw the likeness, so would everyone else around him for twenty years would have noticed it. I was frozen to the spot but didn't have time to think before the Limos came cruising out of the inner yard and parked in line right in front of our little 'love nest.' The chauffeurs all got out to smoke and some even to 'take a pee' up against our sanctuary. They chatted away and I hardly dared to look again but eventually I did. As I said before, the Limos were all Cadillacs but then I noticed something else. The registration numbers were consecutively numbered 1-12 (more cars had arrived by then) and all had the prefix 'SL' except one, the most important one, which had instead the number plate LDR. My first thought was that it was a hire fleet but something told me that it looked like a permanent company fleet. 'SL' I thought, and then it came to me. 'SL' must mean Sidney Lumet the film producer and this was his fleet of Limos. But no, I didn't know Sidney very well but I'd heard that he was a man of modest means who lived for cinema, not clandestine meetings in the dark. I was stumped. Who was the mysterious man and what did 'SL' mean and why was SDL the odd one out? Any ideas?'

Jed and Gina began to speak at once before Jed paused and said 'After you Gina, what do you make of it?' Now Gina paused as if to weigh a momentous thought. 'Stauffenberg.' she said. 'You know that all of those conspirators were buried in unmarked graves don't you and that some leaders were strung up with chicken wire for a slow, and witnessed death? Not Stauffenberg though. It was alleged that he was shot by firing squad but now I'm thinking. Was he? In his case, and with his contacts it's entirely possible that someone took his place in the records and now he's here, maybe master minding this whole affair.'

Author's note; *On July 20th 1944 Klaus Philip Schenk, Count von Stauffenberg was a Lieutenant Colonel and Chief of Staff to General Olbricht which placed him in a good position to attempt Hitler's assassination. The attempt failed and many conspirators were forced to commit suicide or were strung up on meat hooks. Stauffenberg was shot by firing squad 'in the dim rays of the blacked out hooded headlights of an Army Staff car' (Rise&Fall of the Third Reich. William Shirer.)*

Now Jed was shocked. 'It can't be.' he said, 'or if it is, it's just too fantastic and how do you account for him being undetected for so long?'

'I've thought of that,' responded Gina, 'and I've concluded that what Reuben saw tonight would have been very, very rarely seen. It's a kind of uniform, a statement of his authority and personal bravery. He must have been making a very important speech. For the most part, and every day I imagine he might have a glass eye and a prosthetic arm. He'd look like everyone else.' Gina smiled. She had sounded convincing and knew it.

Not to be out done though, Jed had another idea, 'We'll need to do some research in the trial records, if they still exist, but I'm wondering if 'he', the man in uniform, might actually be a 'doppel ganger.' It might be quite a good idea for those who were organising the 'movement' to have the appearance of an heroic and credible figure to lead them and perhaps only a few key people are in on the deception.'

'Well it's no good guessing is it?' responded Gina, 'We've seen SDL before but I don't remember where, but I have got a notion about the fleet of cars. 'SL' she said, 'SL is 'Simpson Line' back in the picture again, now what do you think about that?' 'Maybe, maybe not It's not a competition,' laughed Jed. 'Perhaps we're both right but it doesn't matter much at the moment. Reuben's only half way through his story and that's the important thing to get finalised. Let's carry on tomorrow OK?'

Those missing years 1959-63 (Reuben continues)

I kept a low profile for a time as I found it harder and harder to finish a gig before those gremlins got to me, on stage or anywhere else. Although I had a short stint with Hank Mobley, for the most part I was out of it. I couldn't afford to pay for treatment so I hung about 'Julies' Bar' with all the other winos. I wasn't much use to the 'All America' group either, so my funds began to dry up and there was nothing for it but to dry out.

This had some rather unexpected side effects as I began to read a lot of newspapers that I found in the bins as I rummaged for food. What I mean is that I learnt a lot about the Rev King and the Civil Rights Movement that Dad and Uncle Reuben had been involved with. It kinda opened my eyes as I read about the Montgomery Bus Boycott and Little Rock.

I did know though that 1959 was a very special year in jazz. In the music business we could all feel that something really important was going on. I'll try not to go on about it too much because I wasn't really part of that fantastic year which saw Miles' 'Kind of Blue', Brubeck's 'Take Five,' Mingus's 'Ah Um' and Ornette Coleman's 'The shape of things to come.' Mingus was a 'political' figure with a small 'p'. A year before, he had composed and played 'The Fables of Faubus' an ironic dig at the Governor in the Little Rock Affair. Brubeck refused to tour without his 'black; bass player Eugene Wright, Coleman's work was also about the 'nuclear' age and Miles, well Miles and Coltrane just personified black consciousness. Miles had another asset that wasn't talked about much, and that was the way in which his muted trumpet sound affected the women in the audience. It was said that they blushed from head to toe.

Anyway this brings me to Miss Monroe because she walked in when he was on set one day, and of course just as we were all watching her, she was watching him, and sure enough, there she was, blushing.

Miss Marilyn Monroe. Reuben is Star Struck.

At the end of the evening I was just hanging around the bar when Miss Monroe, I mean Marilyn, came up to me and said, 'Reuben isn't it?' I don't mind telling you I was a bit shocked and surprised that she knew my name. 'Sure is,' I replied, as nonchalantly as I knew how, 'Have you enjoyed the concert tonight?' Her eyes smouldered as if I had discovered her naughty secret, 'Isn't he wonderful,' she sighed, 'Do you know him? I mean do you know him very well?' I didn't but I said yes anyhow.

'Sure I do,' I said, 'We're good buddies Miles and me.' She smiled at me and then said, 'I'd like to meet him. Do you think that you can fix it?' This tack took me by surprise but I could hardly refuse so I said I'd try.

'I'll make it up to you.' she said slipping elegantly off her stool and blowing me a kiss. I was speechless. 'Whisky. Make it a double.' I said.

I decided to fix up a meeting at Dolcilattis and she kind of took to me after that. I suppose she used me to an extent, I found a masseur or a tennis coach for her, sometimes a 'guru' or 'shamen,' she was into that kind of thing. I mean her psychiatrist didn't seem to help much. He just gave her more pills. Nevertheless those were very productive years in her career. 1959 was 'Some like it Hot,' and there was one film at least in each of the next three years starting with 'Let's Make Love,' then it was 'The Misfits,' and the unfinished 'Something's Gotta Give,' in 1962. By then she was in trouble with her contract with Twentieth Century Fox and they replaced her, rather ironically with Kim Novak in 'Kiss Me Stupid.'

So this brings me to 1963, and the months before her death and my arrest. I'll start with the Goodman concert where she appeared with Sam Giancarna the Mafia Boss. BG was invited back to Sam's apartment so a few of us went along as well, but I was keeping a very low profile, well you do when the mob's around, but I couldn't keep my eyes off her. She exuded a kind of sexual energy of which she seemed to be only half aware. As men stared she would just give them the 'girl next door' smile that she had perfected, but it didn't work with the wives of the rich and famous. Take Jackie Kennedy's reaction to 'THAT' dress when Marilyn sang 'Happy Birthday Mr President' for her husband Jack. JFK had said that he could now retire from politics after that rendition 'sung in such a sweet wholesome way,' but Jackie wasn't fooled.

Marilyn made a lot of friends all right but probably more enemies along the way. I'd say that she danced with danger all round as she moved amongst the rich and famous, the straight and the crooked, as well as politicians and pimps.

I couldn't be too concerned about her at this time as I had troubles of my own with Suzy who'd taken a liking to a young man called Leggett who was actually part of that 'All America' crowd. 'Did you say Leggett?' asked Gina. 'We know a Senator Leggett from the STRA reward scheme that we came across before. Any relation?' 'I think so,' replied Reuben, 'Yes I'm sure of it. Big House. Politics. You know. Big man. Now Little Leggett thinks he's a big man too. Suzy gave me a hard time over him and I wouldn't be at all surprised if he set me up at Marilyn's to get his own back. The fact is that I was there that night although I haven't admitted to it. I got this phone call you see, from a 'friend' he said, 'Marilyn was in some bother,' he said and 'I ought to go round.' he said. Well when I arrived I didn't go in but just peeked through the curtains, and as I did so a car pulled up. It was Dr Greenson, her psychiatrist so I hightailed it out of there. I went home and to bed but the next thing I knew it was 6am and the police had come to arrest me. They said that they had information that 'Whitey' was there, meaning me of course. That was my nickname. I got it from playing with many 'white' bands of the day. That's about it. Now get me out of here.'

(Author's note. *There was however, another 'Whitey' on the scene namely Allan 'Whitey' Snyder who was Marilyn's make up artist.*)'

Jed and Gina agreed to call it a night and to carry on the next morning but they were awoken with a telephone call at 6am. It was the police calling to tell them that Reuben had absconded and they had an APB out for him.

'I hope they find him for his sake.' said Gina, 'I think there's a few people out there who'd like to keep him quiet.' It must be scary for him,' said Jed, 'He's found out that you can't trust anybody.' 'Except us' said Gina, 'He's still got us hasn't he?' Jed took her hand gently, 'And I've still got you.' he said, 'and thank God for that. Tell you what Gina this might have given us a bit of time to think things through. I've got my 'play' ready now, just like yours on the Novak case. I think it might open up some possibilities. Would you like to hear it?' Gina thought for a minute then said,' Perhaps it could it start with a hot bedroom scene, say between the 'producer' and the ice cream girl? I've got a costume that's just right.' Jed laughed and held up a Five Dollar bill. 'Vanilla please' he said, as she grabbed the note and ran for the bedroom.

Consuela's Story
(By Jedsy Lomax)

Now it was time for Jed's version of the events surrounding Marilyn's death. Like Gina he had agreed to present the story in a 'fly on the wall' manner. In place of the ubiquitous Edward G Robinson in Gina's 'Novak' story, he had dreamt up 'Cosnsuela Valdes' as Marilyn's maid.

(Author's note. *Marilyn's housekeeper was Eunice Murray but it was Ralph S Greenson, Marilyn's psychiatrist who discovered the body.*)

Scene 1 The flat of Consuela's friend Mary Sanchez.

'I just have to tell someone,' Consuela began, choking back a tear. 'I'm so frightened and I don't know how much or how little to tell the police when they question me. She had so many friends you know and half of them were enemies.' Mary smiled at this apparent contradiction but gently asked her friend to proceed. Mary herself was the widow of the Colombian Ambassador and had met Consuela when she had worked at the Embassy as a cleaner. Despite their different backgrounds they got on very well together although it must be said that Mary was far more sophisticated, refined and knowledgeable about the world. Consuela was homely and holy. She lived to serve others and God. She smiled at her friend and continued. 'The President, the brother, another man, the Italian one, musicians such as Baker and Solidar, actors, including Lawford and Martin, they've all been here and she go there sometime, to their place you know. Reuben told me that she'd had a fling with Miles Davis but I don't believe it. He still 'carried a torch' for that other actress you know, Kim Novak so I wouldn't really trust him as far as Marilyn was concerned. In fact I heard that they were rivals for a part and Reuben got quite cross with her once. I heard them arguing and then she crying. When she went away sometime she come back happy, mostly miserable and sad. One or two time she show me bruise. Doctor come often but she no get better. Lose sparkle and I cry for her.'

Mary moved closer and held her hand, 'There, there,' she said, 'It is very sad, very sad indeed but why are you so worried Consuela. Miss Monroe died of a heart attack or an overdose, so what's worrying you so much?'

Now Consuela burst into a flood of tears that carried on for some time. Each time she tried to speak she cried ad cried again until it seemed that there were no tears left. 'No. No. It can't be,' she cried out, 'she was a very fit young woman you know. It couldn't be a heart attack and I know for sure that she'd been off drugs for some weeks now. In fact she'd been to the Hospital for those pills, you know the ones, the ones that get you off drugs. Methadone I think, yes methadone. She got them a few weeks back and was actually beginning to look better. See, here they are in the bureau, that's where she kept them. 'I'm getting well again Consuela' she said to me each morning as I brought them to her with a glass of water. Here Consuela bit her lip as she opened the bureau drawer and rummaged around amongst a pot pourri of tablets, muttering as she did so, 'Now where are they, where are they?' before turning to Mary with a deep sigh,' They're gone.' she said flatly, 'They were here yesterday, a big bottle. I saw them and now they've gone. Someone's taken them.'

Now Mary was looking concerned, 'Are you sure? Are you absolutely positive Consuela?' she said. 'On the Mercy of the Cross, in Jesus' name and Holy Mary Mother of God I'm certain.' replied Consuela. Mary knew her friend, and that this statement meant more to her than her life so once more she held her hand. 'You're right,' she said, 'It does seem as if you've got something to worry about but just keep this between us at present, maybe until the dust settles a bit. Now was there anything else?'

'Yes,' Consuela continued, 'Mr Kennedy. When Mr Kennedy, that's the younger one you know, Robert left yesterday I could hear them talking or more like arguing. She seemed to be pleading with him and then as he left, he gave her a slip of paper. 'Here,' he said, 'phone this number if you absolutely have to but only in an emergency.' I remember what she said as well. She gave him a hug and a kiss and said, 'Thank you Mr Attorney General.' She liked to cock a snook at people's pretensions and while some thought it funny, others tended to be rather precious about their status in life. Bobby was one of those and he left looking somewhat grumpy. I'd say this though, that Marilyn was no fool. She didn't just 'come out' with words. I mean there was often an intent. Sometimes it was to amuse, maybe to flatter but sometimes there might be a veiled threat as I think there was here. 'I can cause you damage 'she was saying. I know because I've heard her before with Giancarna and others. I know that she put the slip of paper on the bedside table because I saw it there but in the morning it was gone as well, but she did make the call.'

Scene 2 Robert Kennedy's Office

A phone is ringing in an empty office. Soon a man appears and picks it up. 'Mac here.' he says, 'Who is that speaking please?' 'Mac, it's Marilyn,' came the reply, 'Bobby said I could call.' Mac looked worried and put his hand over the mouthpiece to keep it silent even though there was no one else in the room but him. 'He told you not to call here.' he said. 'I just have to talk to him. I must. I'm going crazy. I need . . .' she replied, 'Sure baby you always need,' interrupted Mac, 'No can do. Anyway he's not here.' There was silence until she continued, 'Then get him Mac, get him or, or else, tell him I'm going out of my mind.' Mac refrained from commenting on Miss

Monroe's state of mind but had he detected a threat? What did she mean by <u>or else</u> he wondered.

(Author's note. *Mac is a figment of Jed's imagination but there probably was a 'doorkeeper' of sorts to each of the Kennedys.*)

Mac's considered opinion was that, not only was Monroe unstable, but that she was dangerous as well. Wherever she went she captivated men, mostly in their dreams, but it had been different with his boss and of course, 'his' boss the President. They had not kept their attentions to seductive images on the silver screen, far from it and now he sensed danger. There were many who could make trouble over these 'personal' affairs including the Mafia, the 'Teamsters' Union, Castro, the KGB, political enemies and even political 'friends,' so Mac saw it as his job to keep the lid on any 'inconveniences,' no matter what it took to do so. However he was a careful man and knew that it was best to deal gently with Marilyn at this time. He'd have to see about later if it came to it.

'OK Miss Monroe,' he said, lying through his teeth, 'I'll arrange for him to see you. How would next Wednesday do?' 'No. No. No.' she cried out in desperation, 'it won't do at all. It's got to be now, today. Tell him to come round or else I'll come round to his place tonight. Tell him.'

Mac heard the desperation in her voice. He also heard those two little words again, 'or else.' Now he was worried. 'Sure thing,' he replied, 'I'll see he gets the message but can anyone else help in the meantime?'

She seemed to calm down a bit and even a bit deflated, as if she'd put everything into her plea. 'Thanks Mac you are an angel you know. Yes, call Peter for me and call Dr Greenson. I need to talk to someone.' 'I'll do that right away,' he replied, 'Now you get some rest now.' He put down the phone with a sigh and then picked it up again. 'Call Hoover.' he said, 'Then call Dr Greenson. Tell them both to meet me here at Six pm, and oh yes, place a call to Peter Lawford. Say I called but it wasn't urgent.'

Author's note. *Hoover was head of the FBI. Greenson was Marilyn's psychiatrist and 'Peter' was Lawford, whose first wife had been the Kennedy's sister. He was a well known but maybe not a top billing actor, and part of the Sinatra, Davis, Martin Rat Pack.)*

Scene Three. Consuela's House

After her long chat with Mary, Consuela was glad to get home. She lived alone in a downtown suburb of the Brentwood District in LA not far from Marilyn. It was a small place but neat and tidy like Consuela herself. She kept herself busy at home, at work or at St Patrick's Mission Church where she did the flower arranging with Sister Bridget from the convent.

She had not been home long when she heard a car draw up outside and she was very pleasantly surprised to see Father Martini with two men in dark suits get out. 'Very thoughtful,' she thought as she quickly tidied a few papers before opening the door. 'Oh Father,' she said, 'I'm so pleased to see you. She wasn't Catholic you know but now she's in heaven with the Almighty I'm sure. Please come in and I'll make tea.'

The three men came into the room so far without saying a word. Well there hadn't been time so far, but when she returned with a tray of tea, biscuits and some home made cakes, Martini spoke up. 'Bless you Consuela. You really are the finest of women, cakes too. God bless you.'

The next few moments were taken up in tea pouring and cake munching and then one of the other men spoke. 'Thank you Signora you have been most kind. I am Lucca Bernardi and this is Signor Rainier. We are but small persons doing our best to spread the Gospel and of course we rely many others to help us.' Consuela wondered what this might be about, probably funds she thought. The Church seemed to have an endless need for funds but she never refused. 'Just wait a moment,' she said, 'I'll get my purse. It's only in the kitchen.' but she was stopped in her tracks as she made to get up. 'No. No.' Bernardi said, 'what I meant to say is that we rely on many others to help us in particular ways. For example Father Martini promotes our work and, yes it must be said he does fund raising too. But others help in whatever way they can such as Mayor Tosca, he can oil the planning processes, and Mr Giancarna, well he can help us with the Unions or political problems. You see everyone can do their bit and now we've come to ask you to do yours. Perhaps Father Martini will explain in a little more detail.' Saying which he turned to the Reverend Father who, it must be said, seemed rather reluctant to take the lead.

Nevertheless, making a sign of the Cross, he began. 'Bless you Consuela. Bless you. This is a very distressing time for you we know, but to be frank there are some matters that must be attended to without delay so that no harm is caused to others caught up in Miss Monroe's death. Not to put too fine a point on it I'm talking about Signora Giancarna. I'm sure you will agree that she should not suffer on account of her husband's 'imperfections' (he stressed the word before continuing). You see there may be some letters or mementos, maybe personal things that would only cause her much heartache so we'd like you to find them so that we can take care of it. We would be most grateful. Do you think that you can help us?' Now Consuela may be rather naïve in some respects, but she knew what they were getting at. She was to find any incriminating papers etc and she would be well paid for her trouble. She felt shocked however that it was Father Martini making the offer, although she sensed that he might be under pressure also. 'I'll do what I can,' she said, 'please call tomorrow, say about 6pm after Mass, would that be all right Father?' She knew that this was rather mischievous but she wanted to see if he squirmed with a bad conscience or smiled with the air of a Saint. His eyes dropped to the floor and she had her answer without a word said.

Author's note. *Since the days of Father Coughlin it was not unusual to find the Catholic Church in these situations where their protection of Mother Church against 'Forces of the Devil,' including Communism and, by association, Civil Rights led them into dubious company.*

The men finally got up to leave but, as they approached the door, the other man, Rainier spoke up. She immediately determined that he was the most important of the three as he said, 'Please do not mention our visit to anyone. I promise you that would not be a good idea. Now in confidence I tell you another thing. There is also correspondence about Miss Monroe's contract with Twentieth Century Fox and the fact that Kim Novak was replacing her in a film called 'Kiss me Stupid,' well Sam. I mean Mr Giancarna may have made some rather unwise remarks about what might happen if that went ahead. You know, he was just protecting Miss Monroe but it could be awkward do you see? Just find the papers and we'll sort them out, nothing for you to worry about. Good day.' Consuela saw them out and then called Mary. 'Ginnettis Cafe' she said, 'Ten minutes?' Mary said yes at once, questions could come later.

Scene Four Ginnettis Café

'So that's it,' concluded Consuela when she finished her story, 'Now what do you think I should do?' Mary didn't know what to say but she put up a brave face for her friend. 'As I see it,' she said, 'you might just 'find' a few letters and hand them over. The rest you give to me and I'll keep them safe.' 'You'd really do that, for me?' said Consuela obviously deeply moved. 'It's the least I can do.' replied Mary, 'between you and me I think that they've got the right guy, Solidar. Opportunity and motive; cut and dried. Now let's have tea.'

Scene Five Mary's flat

'Is that the lot?' asked Mary as Consuela handed over a large bundle of papers. 'Yes it is and I'm so glad to be rid of them,' she said. 'Now I must rush or I'll be late for Mass.' Mary heard the door latch click and she looked out to see her friend hurrying up the road to share Mass with Father Martini. She laughed and picked up the phone. 'Is that you Lucca? (Bernardi) Good. Tell Rainier and Martini not to worry because I've got the papers.' she said, and then replaced the receiver at once. She felt sorry for Consuela. Martini would be missing Mass tonight. FIN.

Jed finished his story with a flourish and turned to Gina with a smile. 'There,' he said, 'Now what do you think of that?' 'Well it's a heck of a story,' replied Gina, 'let's hope they catch up with Reuben soon so we can hear his account. Now how about some more ice cream, you know me, one's never enough and you owe me one remember?' saying which she slid softly into his arms as he sat on the settee. Funny he thought how their lovemaking had become so effortless and natural, not like before with other girls when it often seemed to be a tricky affair, sometimes prone to misunderstandings and umbrage if he wasn't careful. Yes, it was good with Gina but could he keep her at arm's length, indeed should he?

Fortunately Reuben was picked up a few days later but had to go into 'rehab' immediately so a further meeting was out of the question for now. Instead they decided to trawl through all the accounts from the newspapers to glean the facts surrounding Marilyn's death. Such a summary would then be the benchmark against which Reuben's account (when they got it,) could be measured. This is what they found out.

Author's note Marilyn's body was officially 'found' at her Brentwood home by Dr Greenson and Eunice Murray at 445 am on 5/8/1962.

The LA County Coroner Dr Thomas Noguchi stated that Marilyn's death was caused by 'acute barbiturate poisoning' and was a 'probable suicide.' The Head Coroner Dr Theodore Curphey elaborated on this saying that Nembutal and Chloral Hydrate were the pills taken.

The first police officer on the scene (Jack Clemmons) believed her to have been murdered noting that there was no glass for taking tablets and no running water at the house at this time. He had been called at 4.45 am by Dr Greenson who told him that she had died from an 'overdose of pills.'

Further investigation was halted because photos/samples 'went missing.'

Robert Kennedy had visited her on that very day but the last time that Marilyn was actually known to be alive was at 745 pm when Peter Lawford telephoned. He later said that she had been 'incomprehensible' and his later call was not answered.

The housekeeper Eunice Murray had actually phoned Dr Engleberg (M. Doctor) soon after midnight when she failed to get an answer from Marilyn's room. He had come to the house and together they had smashed a window for access and found her dead, but neither called the police or paramedics for at least a further 4 hours. However Marilyn's agent A.P. Jacobs had been alerted and left a concert at 10 30pm.

As they studied this short summary (from various sources) Jed turned to Gina and said, 'Leaving aside who had a motive for the moment, it seems that there was opportunity at least between the hours of 745 and midnight so where was Reuben during that time, that is if he can remember.'

Gina agreed, adding that there were other questions too, such as, 'Who called Jacobs, why was Kennedy there, and why did Lawford telephone?'

'I don't know about those but our main job is to get Reuben's story before he forgets everything.' replied Jed, 'Perhaps some of these other questions will come out in the wash don't you think?' She did, but it was a further two weeks before Reuben was recovered enough and lucid enough to talk and this is what he told them.

'Marilyn and Me'. Reuben gets more realistic

This time Reuben seemed to understand the predicament that he was in and began to go over his involvement with some seriousness.

Last time we spoke (he said) I gave you the low down on those Kenton/Novak years and I mentioned Marilyn, how we met and so on. Sure I was on dope and I needed to feed the habit with extra dollars but I was making good money from music as well. There just never seemed to be enough so I guess I was easy prey for guys who wanted to use me. I must admit that I just didn't care who got hurt if I could get my 'fix.' But I'm innocent Jed, I'm innocent but I can't prove it. I mean it, you've 'gotta' help me or I'm toast. So let me tell you about that week.

It was a lovely August, the sun was out and it was just a month since all the parties on Independence Day. Nobody could see what was on the cards, at least not me. Sure I loved Marilyn but not like that if you see what I mean. She cared for me as well I think, teased me you know but we weren't lovers. She just liked to have me around, reminded her of Miles I think and I don't know what really went on there, if anything.

I suppose you could say that they both 'played the field' in their own way but Marilyn's playing field was a lot more hazardous, what with the Kennedy's, Giancarna and maybe others. She was what JFK said she was, a homespun girl who just wanted to be loved and to be happy in her marriages (pity they didn't work out). However her other driving force was not only to be successful but respected too. That was her tragedy.

Perhaps she didn't understand some men. As I said she liked to have me around and that suited me what with Suzy and all. But others took her friendly 'Orange' signs as a 'Go' or even a 'GoGoGo!' but she just smiled her beguiling smile. I mention this because there were two characters hanging around at this time, one was a masseur (at least he said he was) name of Massey, Gus I think. She probably admired his 'pecs' but kept it firmly at a professional level as far as I could see, but he would try it on. 'The towel a little further down please Miss Monroe, how can I do my job like this?' he'd say. Well she'd just smile sweetly and move it maybe 10 centimetres. The other was a different case entirely, studious, like her ex-husband Arthur Miller and maybe that's what appealed in that direction. His name was Simpson, a rather creepy character but she liked him to read to her, Steinbeck especially.

Marilyn wasn't political but she did like to please and I do know that she had agreed to attend a Civil Rights rally later in the week. 'The boys need my support.' I heard her say. Like a hole in the head, I thought. There were those who would try to stop her on both sides of the fence you might say, 'Camelot' (The Kennedys) for the embarrassment she might cause and any of a diverse range of racist groups who would see this as condoning integration which was of course anathema to them. The studios and their backers in organised crime might not like it much either as they struggled to maintain 'squeaky-clean' Doris Day type movies.

But whoever it was would need a fall guy and that's where I would come in. Frustrated black 'druggie' with motive (rejection) and opportunity, yes I told you that I'd been there but not in the house I swear. That's about all I can tell you. Looks bad doesn't it? (Here Reuben sat down)

Commitment and Revelation

'It certainly doesn't look good.' said Gina, 'but it's all circumstantial isn't it? They can't prove anything can they? Just be patient they're bound to drop the charges soon. It's probably just a smokescreen I would think.'

'I agree' said Jed, 'but that doesn't let us off the hook Gina, remember it's not only Reuben's innocence that's at stake because we vowed to expose those 'shakers and movers' behind the scenes who make this kind of thing possible. We're not so far away from those burning crosses down in Alabama thirty years ago, and those that caught up with Reuben's Uncle Reuben in LA in 1942 but this time bigotry has gone underground. However I'm sure that we're getting closer to the men behind the masks and we've accumulated a great deal of evidence over the years. Once Reuben gets discharged I'd like us to go over all that, see where we stand and maybe bring in some help. Do you agree?' Gina was thoughtful for a moment, as if she'd been given a life sentence. 'It'll never end you know,' she said wistfully, 'and who could we possibly trust anyway? But I agree let's do what we can while we can. Deal?' 'Deal' said Jed holding her hand warmly as another took their hands between his. 'Deal.' said Reuben. 'Now there's three of us, Musketeers unite!'

As Gina had forecast the Police could not hold Reuben for much longer without charge and, as soon as he was free he took up his music again with a new-found enthusiasm, this time leading his own 'Solidarity' group. Jed and Gina went to see him perform at the 'Top Nite Spot' and sure enough he was playing better than ever.

They sat through the first half that ended with that wistful Miles Davis piece 'All Blues' to considerable applause. Immediately Reuben strolled over and sat down at their table, 'Hello you cats,' he said. 'What's cooking?' 'Not much' replied Gina, 'I'd just like to say how well you look and how well you're playing.' Reuben smiled as if he had a secret, 'Well it's all down to Suzy you know, brought me back to life and has kept me off drugs ever since.' He waved to a group in the corner, 'Over here,' he said, 'come and meet my friends Jed and Gina.' It was dark and rather crowded so they didn't get a sight of Suzy until he was at their table. 'Jed, Gina, meet my very good friend Jimmy Soo. Soozy this is Jed and Gina who never lost faith in me during those dark days.'

Speechless? You could say so, but Jed and Gina got to their feet at once and shook Jimmy by the hand. 'This is great,' said Jed, 'Now who's for a drink?' 'Scotch for me, and milk for my friend.' said Jimmy with a smile as he sat down at the table. The interval went on and on but finally it was time for Reuben's second set and Soozy left to join other friends. Now it could be said but who would be first? Jed and Gina grinned at one another like Cheshire cats. 'You first.' he said. Gina bubbled with a mixture of bewilderment and pleasure. 'Why didn't he tell us? Why didn't he tell the police? Surely they wouldn't have brought charges if they'd known. But why didn't he tell us?' Jed went serious for a moment before taking her hand gently. 'I don't suppose we'll ever know,' he said, 'but if your life has been persecution on one level, who could blame him for avoiding another? And what about Jimmy? Maybe he wanted it to remain a secret too. Maybe it was family, maybe work, who knows. I must admit it would have made life easier for us by removing suspicions but, when push comes to shove, could we have kept his secret when we saw what danger he was in?' 'No, I think you're right Jed, he's so used to trusting no one he couldn't trust us and he was probably right.'

'End of story.' said Jed, 'Hurrah for Hollywood and all that. Let's go home and then, how would you like another week at the Georgian in Santa Monica? I want to practise my Clark Gable again, this time the scene where he picks her up and carries her up the stairs.' 'Oh no, I shall scream,' laughed Gina, 'but not until later maybe. Come on let's go.'

'Not so fast baby,' he said, drawing her close, 'Remember that when Brett has got Scarlet pinned to the bed that it's you Gina, that I'm making love to and the one that I love' 'Yes Rhett I know,' she replied cheekily.

End Of Part Three

PART FOUR
'HYDRA'

London 1827
Charleston 1822
Montmartre 1848
1848-51
Charleston1860
The Civil war 1861-5

Jed and Gina had committed themselves to unmask the shadowy figures who seemed to organise and co-ordinate racist activity throughout the US and elsewhere. They had much work to do to understand the origins of the groups such as the 'Covenant' and the 'Consortium' that they had come across. But there was time for that.

Then one night, as they settled down together on the settee to watch a late night movie, they both seemed to feel drowsy as the screen flickered before them as if with a faulty signal. Then, as it cleared, they could see that the film that came on the screen was different to the one that they expected. They sat mesmerised, even hypnotised as it began.

TWENTIETH CENTURY FOX PRESENTS

HYDRA

A tale of intrigue over a hundred years from 1770-1870

Featuring George Sanders, David Niven and Sidney Poitier.

Introducing **MISS MARILYN MONROE** as Effie.

And starring

CLARK GABLE AS HUGH DE RAINIER

This film has an X Certificate.

Scene One. Walpole's Coffee House in Regent Street London in 1827

The Film now begins with a scene set in a Coffee house. A caption reads 'REGENT STREET LONDON IN THE YEAR 1827.' The music is appropriately, Schubert's 'Trout Quintet,' begun eight years earlier. Three men are seated at a table with newspapers strewn before them as a fourth approaches. 'Here he is,' says one. 'They say he's always late,' whispers another,' and 'Shsh he'll hear you.' says the third. The newcomer is the American whom they are expecting and, as he gets close they can see that he is in the company of a very lovely young blonde.

There are gasps in the room as she manoeuvres her way past tables, and threads her ample figure rather voluptuously through the room. She is covered from head to toe in a long brown Beaver fur coat, but for many there she might just as well have been naked. Twinkling beneath the hem of the coat are two high heels that seem to sparkle in the dim lights.

The three men at the table stand to receive their guests shaking them both warmly by the hand. 'Welcome, welcome,' says the first man, 'welcome to our humble home.' He says this with a laugh that seems to break the ice and they all sit down. 'I'll order Coffee,' says the second, getting up to leave the table. 'And I'll help.' says the third, thus leaving the visitor, his host and the girl alone. 'I'm Sir James Cotton.' says the host, 'I'm a nephew of the Tory leader (*Cotton was related*) so we do have some influence there, but the agenda's pretty well set by Cobbett and his fellow travellers in the Whig Party. I'm the one who invited you over, and we're hoping that you can tell us how you dealt with the situation in 1822 in the States. You don't know what we're up against here. It's a hotbed of reformers and radicals on every street corner so we have to be very careful.'

'Well I'll do what I can' replied his guest 'as you know I'm Rainier, or more precisely Hugh de Rainier, second generation Monegasque now living in Charleston. And this is Effie, a bright girl too, she's the granddaughter of George Mason of Virginia and her husband is Cyrus Simpson the ship owner. He's here on business but up in Liverpool I think and she's keeping me company for now aren't you ma cherie?'

He spoke in a kind of Southern drawl with definite French inflexions as he smiled at her fondly. 'Mais oui m'sieur.' she said.

Authors note. *After Independence was secured in 1770 politicians argued long for their ideal of how the new nation would be governed. Alexander Hamilton stood for a single authority and Mason for largely Independent States but the compromise of James Madison won the day.*

Rainier's reputation went before him. Although still very young he was recognised as a leader in the political world in which he lived.

In this regard he was following in his father's footsteps who had been an equerry to Louis XV1 then, sensing the game was up had served in the Napoleonic army at the Battle of Waterloo in 1815. Defeat there persuaded him to move to Quebec where, despite Wolfe's victory in 1759, there remained a solid French majority some from the 'Ancien Regime' of the executed Louis, and this suited Rainier well. Later he moved the family to Charleston where other independent minded folk were known to be active, this time amongst the new 'Americans.' Here he would found a new 'dynasty' with generations of Rainiers leading the cause of Anglo Saxon hegemony throughout the world. This was a good town for those with shipping interests and it was there that he had met Simpson, already a considerable operator in the slave trade. They had then become partners and the driving force behind the 'American Colonisation Society' established in 1822, in their words, but not widely publicised, 'to rid the US of it's racially undesirable Afro-Americans.'

Authors note. *The society was formed with those intentions in 1822. Later many, so-called 'returnees' were transported at the end of the Civil War.*

Simpson had joked that they had made money, taking Africans to America, and now could make money taking them back. 'That's known as a 'Full House,' Rainier had said in reply. The two got on well.

The other two men in the Coffee house were Sir Edmund Lisle, a distant cousin of King George 1V and Alexander Hamilton the Duke of Hamilton. When these two had returned, some coffee drunk, and a pipe or three smoked, Rainier began to speak. 'Now let me explain how it was with us back in 1822.' he said, 'because that's why I'm here isn't it? Well, imagine a warehouse at the dockyard in Charleston. Not far away is the 'Slave Mart' where buyers and sellers negotiate prices on the 'merchandise' just arrived from West Africa. Gathered there are a group of men. Farmers and others, business or professional types, but nearly all with an interest in the slave trade. For many their economic life depends on it. My father, now deceased (God rest his soul,) stands to speak.'

Scene Two. Charleston Docks 1822.

'Gentlemen and ladies, for I see that there are a few, thank you, thank you for being here today as we begin a new chapter in this nation's history. Today we launch the 'American Colonisation Society,' with the long-term aim of ridding this country of those racially undesirable blacks who would dominate us if they could.(*ref. Africa. Curtin*) Of course at present we are dependent on their labour as slaves and as slaves they must remain. Those seeking, securing, or being granted their freedom, will no longer hold any right to be resident here, but we do have a plan for them.

To that end we have purchased land in West Africa at a place called Monrovia and the new 'Simpson Line' has already begun shipments, on a voluntary basis for the present. What we need now is money. We need your dollars please to make this venture possible, because I warn you that if we do not act now it could be too late. There are those who already smell gunpowder following the recent decision on the 'Missouri Compromise Line' and I don't need to remind anyone about the tragedy in Haiti but a few years ago (1793) when, as many of you know, my brother, his wife and all their little children were killed in the slave revolt led by that renegade Toussaint L'Ouverture, and thousands of others too.

Up until recently I would suggest there had been a great deal of optimism that our way of life might be preserved and even enhanced, but that's not the case now and there is need for a fight back starting today. We all know that the success of our Southern States depended on two cash crops, cotton and sugar. I'd say that we had a modest labour force of slaves at first but when Whitney's cotton gin and Bore's sugar vats were introduced, production was able to be increased maybe tenfold and of course demand for slaves rose too. Add in the introduction of the light draft steamboats, thanks to my friend Simpson, and a burgeoning economic future beckoned. Our neighbours are jealous of our success and, mark my words they are out to take all that we have. We'll need help, possibly from France unless the 'radicals' continue to make a come back there. In essence, our fight is the fight for survival of any superior racial species if they become threatened by an inferior one.

Authors note. *Jefferson said that he considered the Missouri Compromise (1819) to be the' death knell of the Union' allowing, as it did, the slave state of Missouri into the Union. To achieve balance, Maine was admitted as a 'free' stat, but legislation also introduced the prohibition of slavery north of latitude 36.30. This became a battle line in the Civil War.'*

(ref. America. Alistair Cooke)

This cannot be a local affair, gentlemen. We have already sent agents to all areas in the country so that we will be ready when the time comes. We have sent emissaries to other countries too and although we may have to suffer some reverses on the way, our commitment is clear. We will never surrender our way of life to an inferior race. We must be patient and above all we must keep our operations and intentions secret. It may be that we will hold common cause with others from time to time, and maybe another leader will emerge on the world stage who would make these things possible but for now it's up to us. Are you with us?'

At this invocation everyone present got to their feet and clapped vigorously. Then a young boy began to sing as if in the Hebrew Chorus, 'Lead us, lead us, lead us.' Soon, the song was taken up by the entire crowd as louder and louder they sang, 'Lead us, LEAD US, **LEAD US**.'

Rainier stood for a moment then, with a wave he stepped off the stage and out into the sunlight at the back of the warehouse. He smiled, he was satisfied, it had begun and it would never stop, he was sure of it.

Scene three. Back in Walpole's coffee house that same day in 1827.

Rainier finished his story with a smile. 'And I'm proud to tell you,' he said, 'that I was that young boy, 16 then, 21 now and, since my father's death, the leader of the group. My son will follow me, and then his son will lead until we have achieved our aims, even if it takes a hundred years. You can help us and we can help you. Now tell me what you need.'

Lisle spoke first. 'It seems to me,' he said, 'that all our fortunes are tied up in the slavery business, and I use the word 'fortunes' advisedly. For my own part my family have sugar plantations throughout the West Indies and I must say that they afford us a good living, based on slavery of course. Our latest project has been the complete rebuild of Barrington Court the family home near Crewkerne in Somerset and we have a mind to go further. All of this will be thrown into disarray if Wilberforce gets his way. Our friends in Bristol and Bath are in a similar position'

Author's note. *Barrington Court is now a National Trust property with much evidence on show about the 'Lisle' connection. Wilberforce campaigned actively during the 1780's but slavery in the British Empire was not abolished until 1834.*

'And what will happen to those freed slaves I ask you? We must prevent them from coming here at all costs so we need another option, perhaps the colony in Sierra Leone that was set up for the 'black poor of London' back in 1787. We could send our 'returnees' there if the government had the will. And if not it would have to be 'Our Enterprise' as in America.'

Rainier was impressed. This is what he wanted to hear and he murmured his approval before turning to Hamilton. 'And you sir,' he said, 'what is your view on the matter in hand?' Hamilton thought for a moment before he made his reply. 'Gentlemen, and lady of course,' he said as he bowed in her direction, 'it seems to me that you have described the 'externals' of our dilemma very well so I'll turn to the 'internals,' namely who runs this damned country of ours and in whose interest? The liberal agenda is going too far and, mark my words, it won't be long before we have fully legalised Trade Unions here. Our power base, including slavery options, working hours, conditions, pay and who to hire will have to be the basis of negotiation in which we are not guaranteed to come out on top. So it's vital that we stop the rot now before it's too late.'

Author's note. *UK Trade Unions were legalised that same year in 1827.*

Rainier, although a visitor, seemed to be chairing the meeting and he spoke again, very warmly but with authority to those present.

'We are but a few here and now,' he said, 'but I am confident that there are many who think like us and crave for leadership, and it is that that my organisation will provide, this year, next year, and into eternity if necessary. You must begin with your own version of the American precedent. I suggest you call it the 'Anglo African Society' for now.

Authors note *The AAS was so founded in 1827.*

I hope that you won't find my next proposal too dramatic because what I have to tell you must be protected unto death. It is that critical and it is this. We have created an organisation in the United States that will bring about white hegemony in our Anglo Saxon homelands.

We call this organisation HYDRA and we have named it after the nine-headed creature from Greek mythology, so we too will have nine heads. The US and Canada are secured and you are to be the third followed by France, Germany and the Benelux countries plus Southern Africa and Australia/New Zealand. As a matter of form now I'm going to ask you to swear an oath and to exchange, let's say some bodily fluid. Not blood, it wouldn't be appropriate here would it?' he smiled, 'No, I suggest that we all eat from the same biscuit here on the table and that we all drink from the same cup of coffee thereby mingling our saliva for ever. We will then voice our commitment to the cause together in these simple words.

'We are Hydra but we will never mention this word again. We commit ourselves on pain of death to be ready to serve, and never betray our leader now and forever. This land is ours, this land is not theirs.'

The ceremony over and their guests departed, the three men looked at each other rather dumbfounded before Lisle put their thoughts into words.

'He's either mad or a genius,' he said, 'anyway it seems that we've signed up to some secret society, 'communion' and all.' With that they too left the coffee house where life went on as before, but not for them.

Scene Three. A café in Montmartre in May 1848

Rainier is seated at the café 'Miquelon' with three others. It is 21 years since he had added the United Kingdom to the many-headed Hydra, and every other country except France had joined during those years despite his many efforts. He considers this to be an important year and an important month, in which he might well achieve his objective of bringing the French nation into the 'Hydra' fold as the ninth head. For this to come about he needs a government sympathetic to his aims, namely a counter-revolutionary one where liberal ideas of anti slavery etc would not be countenanced; but neither the 'Ultra' party of Artois under LouisXIII, nor Charles X had shown any interest, and Louis Philippe was too liberal to consider Rainiers prospectus. Then in February 1848 his worst nightmare comes true, as Louis Philippe is overthrown by hard line men of the left with radical social ideas, such as Ledru Rollin. There is a desperate need for action and it has to be now.

Authors note *Since the French revolution in 1789 and the final abdication of Napoleon Bonaparte in 1815, France had' see-sawed' between those with true revolutionary zeal and those who supported a return to the 'Ancien Regime' in some form or other. Successive Kings had failed to find a 'middle way' and this had led to riots and the accession of Louis Philippe in 1830 as 'the heir to the revolution.' However even this did not satisfy the radicals and soon they were on the streets again in February 1848 ushering in a 'Provisional Government' of a true revolutionary character aiming to abolish slavery and introduce universal suffrage.* (Alfred Cobban)

Rainier has done well in his choice of guests, all of whom are supporters of Louis Napoleon Bonaparte in whom Rainier had high hopes. The 'left' is disorganised and this could well be an opportunity for a strong leader who might welcome the Hydra concept of white supremacy.

Firstly there is Louis' mistress the beautiful (and wealthy) 'Miss' Howard, later to become Comtesse de Beauregarde, then there is Albert Montalambert who represents a 'deal' with the church and lastly Victor Hugo the celebrated novelist whose writings can make or break any ambitious politician. Rainier is hoping that they will convince Louis to back Hydra when he becomes President or, perhaps Emperor.

Authors note. *These three were known to be amongst his followers.*

'Madame.' he begins, 'Madame. I am so honoured that you have agreed to meet with us this day. I don't need to tell you that the next months will be crucial. Louis will need your support of course and money will help, it always does doesn't it? Gentlemen, thank you also, I know that you are aware of the timeliness of this meeting. To put it bluntly I can get Louis elected and God knows he must be. However to obtain my considerable influence I would wish to have a firm commitment to the implementation of the Hydra policies that I outlined to you before this meeting. The situation in Paris has become desperate as you know and. if we agree I am prepared to put money and resources of manpower, arms and transportation at his command. It's barely three months since that rabble of Ledru and the others took control of both houses and look what they've done already. We now have nine million French peasants to deal with instead of less than a million as a result of the new electoral franchise, and what's worse is the abolition of slavery on which much of the world economy depends. I predict disaster in our colonies. Fortunately our opponents are men of principle and they have promised to hold an election in June and that will be our opportunity. I can tell you that that is the last thing I would do in their shoes and I hope that Louis will feel the same if he ever gets the chance. So what do you think?'

It was Hugo who spoke first, 'I agree it looks bad at present but let's see if Louis wants to stand first, he's been cautious in the past as you know. I may well lend him my 'pen' for now but be aware that I will not hesitate to be a 'critique' should he venture beyond his legitimate authority.'

'Miss' Howard spoke next. 'He is brave my Louis but he's no fool. He has seen so many tumbrels rolling and heads rolling in the past that he has learned to be cautious, but he will be with you if there is some certainty of success. He may need advice and the arms and transport that you mention especially if he needs to consolidate his power in a few years.

If so I am sure he will consider your proposal.'

Rainier was far from pleased at this reply, 'I demand an agreement Madame, a concordat if you like, in writing Madame. It must be a commitment on his behalf signed by him.'

'Madame' Howard flushed. She was not used to being spoken to in that manner. 'Demand, demand you say? Vous etes un idiot! We do not give in to blackmail and as far as I am concerned that is the end of the matter,' And with that she got up to leave pausing only to bow to the three men present; but before she had taken a pace forward Montalambert stepped in front of her with a big smile. 'Madame,' he said, 'that man is too blunt I agree but you haven't heard from me yet. I will state the position of the Church in all this so please sit and hear me out, and if you still feel the same, leave then.' The lady seemed suitably mollified and smiling graciously she sat down but added a barb at Rainier as she did so. 'I have a really important engagement at three with my hairdresser,' she said rather mischievously 'so I don't want to be delayed by any more threats. Now that really is important business.'

It was now up to Montalambert to save the day and this is what he said.

'The Church will always back the forces of law and order. We will have no truck with lawless peasants on the streets, so it is likely, nay almost certain that we will lend our support to Louis Napoleon. There is a new element too with the writings of Marx inflaming the crowds with talk of 'communism,' and he is here in Paris. What's more, religion itself is under threat and we will defend it to the last, as you would expect. There was a time when Kings were servants of the Pope, and Oh that it might be so again. That sacred link was broken back in 1814 when Louis Philippe declared that Catholicism was no longer the religion of the State. As I said, the Church stands for a settled way of life, and we acknowledge that the white man brings order, decency and civilisation to the world. The black man is a child and would rebel if he could, so we would agree with the 'Hydra' philosophy that this balance must be maintained at all costs. And note my friends that this black 'savage' now has not one but three places to look to for support. We know about the soft liberals of our world, but now we must add in the forces of Islam so recently defeated by our gallant forces in Algeria. And what of the third element? Yes, the words of Karl Marx and his communist ideas. I predict that these forces will come together to challenge our way of life all too soon. They will not subside either, and it may be that the vigilance of 'Hydra' may be needed well into the next century, maybe here and maybe elsewhere.'

Rainier was pleased with these words and turned apologetically to 'Miss' Howard. 'He puts it so much better than me Madame. Please accept my humble apologies and tell your, um, tell Louis that we shall be pleased to hear from him soon.' The lady now arose once more and with one word she left the room. 'Attendez' (wait) she said as she 'bustled' out.

The film continues

The next scenes show how Rainier's objectives for Hydra in France are finally achieved through the accession of Louis to the throne. Hydra finally has its' nine heads, and the work of co-ordination can begin.

Paris 1848

The date 1848 hovers over the screen as this section shows riots on the streets superimposed over names too numerous to mention as we see the Army, aided by a vanguard of militia with large H (signifying Hydra) finally overcoming resistance of the Provisional Government at the barricades. Louis Napoleon is victorious and finally elected as President of the Council.

Paris 1849

A new date appears on the screen, 1849, as Louis begins a crackdown on the main opposition the 'Solidaritie Republicaine,' ushering in wider repressive legislation and new rights for the church, 'le Loi Falloux'.

Paris 1850

1850 looms large over scenes as paper is tossed into bonfires as Louis cancels much of PG Govt legislation including universal suffrage.

Paris 1851

The date 1851 is shown dripping in blood as Louis dissolves the Assembly and puts 30,000 troops on the streets including a strong force of 'Hydra' militia to enforce his will. The barricades are there again and Victor Hugo forms a committee of resistance as he said he would, but to no avail. Louis is eventually declared Emperor Napoleon III and Rainier is very pleased with his work as 'Mrs' Howard personally delivers the hand-signed commitment of intent from the new Emperor.

The film now shows a sea journey back to the United States as Rainier and others travel back, having become very concerned about developments there. They have read of the news that Kansas and Nebraska have decided that individual states could decide on slavery issues, and although this was encouraging, much attention was given to the exploits of one John Brown, a staunch Unionist whose raid on the 'slaver' settlement at Pottawattie led to a song that resounded through the land in his honour. 'John Brown's body lies a'mouldering in the grave, but his soul goes marching on.' it went. Rainier was worried and thought that he needed to 'direct' affairs once more, but events seemed to go from bad to worse as the election of an anti slavery president loomed.

He finally decided to set up a meeting with Vice President Stephens of South Carolina to confront him with a stark choice.

The Vice President's Office. Charleston December 19th 1860

It would not be accurate to say that Rainier was a welcome visitor in the VP's office. Indeed, since coming to Charleston he had made as many enemies as friends and Stephens, the VP was probably neither. In fact he rather envied Rainier who was by now one of the wealthiest men in the town, having built up his wealth through judicious investments and together with Simpson, secured a virtual monopoly on the slave trade.

So Stephens, a banker, although slightly intimidated by his visitor, put on his most officious tone as he welcomed his guest. 'Come in Rainier,' he said, 'you're lucky I've got time to see you. Busy man you know so let's get on with it. What do you want to see me about?'

Rainier smiled and took his time. He sat down and took out two large cigars offering one across the desk behind which Stephens was taking refuge. 'Smoke?' he said, 'Great Havanas from our plantations there. Do have one Edward.' He now slipped effortlessly into a personal mode of expression that he knew would put Stephens even more ill at ease. 'No, well never mind. Let's hope there'll still be there in a year or two, but the way things are going I fear that our own plantations, and those under sugar or cotton may soon be a thing of the past. That is why I am here.'

Now the penny dropped. Stephens was only too aware that positions on slavery and anti slavery were becoming polarised and only the previous week he had made a speech in which he stated that, 'The Negro is not equal to the white man.' It was well received in Charleston and South Carolina but that was only to be expected of a 'slave' state.

Author's note. *Stephens did make that speech.*

Now he turned to Rainier and said. 'We're all agreed here. We won't be bullied by the Union, or any new 'country boy' President if he's elected next year. So what more do you think we should do?' Rainier replied immediately,' We must strike first, now, actually tomorrow, because that's your last meeting of the State Legislature before the Christmas and New Year holidays. You can't wait for Abe Lincoln to get elected and force his own agenda. Here, I've prepared a statement that I'd like you to agree with the other members tomorrow. Then issue it to the press.'

He now handed over a rather impressive looking document to Stephens who began to read through all the official terms such as, 'Whereas it is true that' and 'notwithstanding the aforesaid' before he came to the central point, no less than a secession from the Union.

Authors note. *The actual words in the South Carolina document of 20ᵗʰ December 1860 were, 'We dissolve the Union now subsisting.'*

Stephens didn't like it. He didn't like it at all. He didn't like the idea and he didn't like Rainier, who he thought was trying to railroad him into a dangerous position. 'I don't see what the rush is,' he said, 'Lincoln might not get in, maybe we'll get a 'dove' with whom we can negotiate. Frankly I'd prefer to leave it.' Rainier looked grim, 'Then look outside your window,' he said menacingly, 'then tell me again what you'll do tomorrow.' Stephens was taken aback. He didn't like it. He didn't like it at all, and especially he did not like what he saw in the courtyard below, for there in neat ranks were maybe one hundred mounted militiamen wearing the 'Eagle' symbol of South Carolina and a large 'H' badge beside it. The H is in black on a white circle within a red square and both are neatly sewn onto their grey uniforms. Stephens turned to Rainier, 'What does this mean?' he said, 'Why are these men here?'

'They're here to accept your resignation or to be the vanguard in the new 'Confederate South Carolina Militia.' replied Rainier, 'they are my own chosen men bearing the H of my Hydra organisation and they'll fight to the death for our homelands. Now choose.'

Stephens chose to present the document to the Assembly, and it was then passed unanimously to loud applause and a vote of thanks to Stephens for his 'bravery.' Rainier was quietly content. He did not seek plaudits. The die was cast and his ambitions for white supremacy were under way.

Authors note. *Lincoln was elected three months later, stating immediately that any secessions from the Union were void. Battle lines were drawn.*

The Civil War 1861-5

Now the film continues with images of war with occasional captions and dates. The first is 'Fort Sumter 1861' followed by 'Antietum 1862' then 'Gettysburg 1863' and the Confederate surrender at Appamatox in 1865.

A curtain closes, the war is over but almost immediately it opens again to reveal a large crowd milling about outside Fords Theatre. There is no sound. It is as if time is suspended. Then a tall man enters the building and takes his seat. A new camera angle shows another man approaching the President's box, for it is he, Abe Lincoln who sits there. A drum roll begins, so quietly as to be almost inaudible but getting louder as the man draws near. Then a shot rings out and the drums reach a crescendo. The President falls to the floor and the man, John Wilkes Booth, escapes.

The curtain closes once more and the camera pans to a figure seated in the audience surrounded by the crowd of theatre-goers, some ecstatic, some distraught. Then gradually the crowd is faded out of the picture and the man sits alone with his head in his hands. We see that it is Rainier seated in a theatre seat in the shape of an H and we can barely hear what he is saying to himself as he begins, 'Quel dommage! What a blunder1!'

Then his voice strengthens as he rises and addresses the empty theatre.'Brothers, Sisters, Ladies and Gentlemen.' he begins, 'I cannot deny that this killing is a major setback. It will 'lionise' Lincoln and much of our cause will be forgotten. Our 'homelands and women will be raped by a vicious invader and carpet-baggers will take all of our most precious possessions. Our slaves will roam free to cause chaos and disorder for decades. But this land is ours, this land is not theirs and from these ashes we will arise once more not only here in the US but also abroad where we have already sown our seeds to good effect. Hydra will go underground, so deep that no one will find us but we will continue to build up our power base in a clandestine way through many organisations. There are some such groups already and we will shortly be forming a new one. They will be called the 'Red Shirts,' but our connection with them will remain a secret. They will operate in Mississippi at first and ensure that freed slaves are not 'encouraged' to take up their voting rights.

Authors note. *The Red Shirts were formed in 1875 as the military arm of the Democratic Party with the aim of 'driving blacks from the polls.'*

The Ku Klax Klan was founded in 1865, the same year as the 'Southern Cross'. The 'Knights of White Camelia' were founded in 1867.

I am confident that each time will find it's own leaders and maybe one who will bring our dream of white supremacy to fruition. Perhaps that will be here or maybe in Europe when conditions are right, when Aryans take on the dark underworld of communism and racial pollution. Be ready now mes amis, but above all train your young. They are our future.'

He sits down. There is no audience. There is no applause. His figure now gradually melts away, and the only image left on the screen as the credits roll is a chair in the shape of an H, as if it will be there forever.

The End of the film

After the film finished this symbol remained as a white light instead of the small white dot that normally stays there until sleepy film watchers wake up. So it was with some surprise that Jed came to and nudged Gina into wakefulness. 'Strange, that light,' he said, 'it seems to be an H. maybe they're advertising a new programme.' To be honest Gina hardly heard him because she was asleep again almost immediately. He carried her carefully into the bedroom and lay down closing his eyes thankfully.

Within seconds he was awake, 'Gina Gina,' he cried out, 'I've just had a terrible dream. Wake up, please wake up.' But Gina seemed to be dead to the world and eventually sleep conquered Jed as well.

In the morning she snuggled up to him and said, 'Did I hear you say you had a dream last night?' Jed lay somewhat dozily beside her. 'Did I?' he said, 'I'm afraid I don't remember. Toast and honey?' Gina smiled the smile of a Cheshire cat, 'Yes please Jed and then DO come back to bed. Funny you know I had a strange dream as well, something about a monster I think. Funny how you forget in the morning isn't it?'

End Of Part Four

PART FIVE
REUBEN'S REVENGE

Muddy Waters

Charleston. South Carolina

Jackson Mississippi

Reuben behind bars again

SOS. Jed and Gina arrive

Oh Mr Porter

The crock of gold

The Hydras lair

The lair itself

Footnote

Before their dream (or nightmare) we had left Jed and Gina still a bit shell shocked after their meeting with Reuben's friend Suzy, or Jimmy Soo, as it turned out. Reuben himself was now by now well established at the 'Top Nite Spot' with his own group, 'Solidarity' but unexpectedly the Club had to close after a drugs 'bust.' Reuben was not implicated but he was out of a job for a time while the club took the police to court over 'planted' evidence. It transpired that the 'evidence' (packs of cocaine) presented to the DA's office were actually sealed in packages unique to the Police Force. The officers responsible were questioned at length by the FBI and finally admitted that they had been in the pay of a 'secret society' that they only knew as 'ALL.'(The American Liberty League) They had been well paid for their services to 'close down that n . . . club.' In this they were successful because it had been a kind of co-operative venture amongst jazz enthusiasts who could not afford to restart it.

Muddy Waters

However Reuben now had a stroke of luck when he received a call from Lou Isaacs from Chess records. Now Reuben was a real optimist, but this was much more than he had expected and he tried not to show his excitement as he waited for Lou to speak. This was just as well because it was actually not at all what he expected, but this time in a good way.

'Reuben,' said Lou, 'we're looking for a band to tour with 'Muddy' (Waters) next month. Sorry it's short notice but we had asked Lee Morgan and he's had to cry off. 'Muddy' has heard that new hit record of Lee and his band, 'Sidewinder' you know and he just loves it. You do that one don't you? It's for six weeks down in the Deep South. Can you do it?' Here Reuben should have given a no and a yes but he decided at once that 'Sidewinder' would be in his repertoire from now on, so he said 'Sure Lou, love to, I'll just have to check out the guys. OK?'

Authors note. *Chess* had been Muddy's recording partners for some time. They were formally called 'Aristrocat Records.' Such a tour might provide 'live' recordings and maybe another hit for Muddy after his famous 'I'm your Hoochie Coochie man.'

Lee Morgan was only 26 at the time but was the hottest new trumpeter on the scene especially after his work with Coltrane. He was shot in 1972. His main rival 'Booker Little' had died of uraemia in 1961.

Charleston South Carolina

Charleston was the first stop on the 'Muddy Waters visits muddy waters' Grand Tour of the Deep South. To follow were Atlanta in Georgia, Birmingham in Alabama, Vicksburg and Jackson in Mississippi, New Orleans in Louisiana, Miami in Florida and Charleston again.

Charleston is called the 'Holy City' because of the many church spires and one of the first things that Muddy did was to sing one of his favourite spirituals in one of the main parks, 'The Corrinne Jones Playground.' It was 'Why don't you live so God can use you,' and Reuben listened spellbound. This time. This time he would do just that he decided.

The concert was to be at the 'Village Playhouse' east of the 'Cooper' river and everything seemed to be in place. Rehearsals had gone well both with the Waters ensemble and 'Solidarity,' including the requested 'Sidewinder,' much to Muddy's delight. Then on the eve of the Concert Reuben heard that 'Lucky' Thomas his keyboard player, who never said boo to a goose, had been 'unlucky' got drawn into a fight and was now in hospital. Fortunately a local agent, Dan Moses found an excellent 'dep' known as 'Roly' Roscoe but Reuben was not happy, suspecting Roscoe of being a racist from his manner and from what he said. Nevertheless the Concert did take place and it was a great success, especially the two features, Muddy's 'Hoochie Coochie Man,' and Reuben's 'Sidewinder'.

Now it was on to Atlanta Georgia, Birmingham Alabama and then Vicksburg in Mississippi before moving on to Jackson. Here they got a two week break just doing informal media work with a few impromptu gigs on the side. Also planned at this time was a 'Mardis Gras' open-air extravaganza in honour of Otis Spann the celebrated blues pianist, who had been born in Jackson and was travelling with the Waters band. Of course Mardis Gras should be in January but no one seemed to mind.

Jackson Mississippi

It was a lovely afternoon in June and Lefleurs Bluff State Park was crammed with visitors, many of them wearing traditional Mardis Gras dress and organised in the traditional 'krews' as in New Orleans. Others just wore a fancy hat or just came as they were. It was that informal.

Reuben felt quite nostalgic because his father and uncle had often told him about the New Orleans parades, and now here he was in one of them, albeit in Jackson. 'Buddy Bolden lives on' he thought to himself. The evening concert was also a great success as, tired but happy, the musicians sauntered their way back to the Madison Hotel where they were staying. But they were in for a nasty surprise as they got closer.

There were three Police Cars neatly parked outside the front of the hotel and all had their blue lights flashing, signifying, it seemed, something of an emergency, or as someone drily remarked, 'The Mayor's out for dinner with the Police Chief.' As it turned out it was neither. You might call it a 'raid' but it was done in a very civilised way, as every musician was quietly led away to separate tables in a large hall to be questioned by plain-clothes police officers (later to be identified as FBI.) Each interrogation began in the same way and this was Reuben's experience.

Officer. 'Name? etc etc. Can you account for your movements, hour by hour over the last two weeks? Do you or have you ever belonged to the Ku Klax Klan? Have you any connections with the NAACP? What do you know about the recent Civil Rights murders?'

Author's note. *Three civil rights activists went missing in Mississipi on 21ˢᵗ June 1964. Their bodies were found some time later. Our story is based around the events of this time, although it does not follow the actual case history, or the story in the film 'Mississipi Burning.'*

<u>Reuben</u> 'As you probably already know, I'm Reuben Solidar and I'm on tour with my band with Muddy Waters. No, I can't give you an hourly account, but I can tell you that we were in Vicksburg two weeks ago and now we're here. I can give you names of hotels if you like. About the murders, well I only know what everyone else has heard on the news. Three civil rights men went missing and have now been found murdered'.

<u>Officer</u> 'Do you know where the bodies were found?'

<u>Reuben</u> 'No idea, none at all.'

<u>Officer</u> 'Would it surprise you then if I told you that it was at Monroe Lake near Vicksburg? Would it surprise you then to know that the coroner says that they probably died two weeks ago? A night you might remember, the night of your concert there in fact. The 21st June.'

Reuben was taken aback. He had experience of the way that some police officers put two and two together and came up five but what was this particular officer suggesting and on what evidence? There were twenty musicians at least on the 'Waters' tour, so were they all under suspicion?

He decided to call the man's bluff so he just said, 'I know nothing about all this. If you have something, charge me.' Unfortunately the reply was not what he expected. The officer just smiled, 'Book him Harry.' he said.

Reuben behind bars again

It didn't take Reuben long to find out that he was the only one being held, 'on suspicion' as the officers put it. According to his interrogators they also had an eye-witness who would testify that he was involved. As to motive they suggested that it may have just been an opportunistic robbery, but more importantly they said that they had evidence that Reuben was a member of the racist American Liberty League (The ALL) and as such would have motive to kill the Civil Rights activists. This put Reuben on the spot because he could hardly deny that he had been in their pay for some considerable time. Of course he said that that was all in the past, and that he had been off drugs and their pay for some years but the officer just smiled and said, 'Is that so?'

Reuben was in trouble. Muddy Waters and the touring party came to see him but could not be of any help before they moved on to New Orleans.

Some like Muddy, were sympathetic, others less so, 'You never know with Reuben and that's a fact.' said one. Fortunately the organisers managed to secure the services of Howard McGhee who was just coming to the end of a tour with the dynamic young pianist, Phineas Newborn. If he joined Muddy's tour, he said, he'd have to bring Phineas with him so Reuben's 'dep' keyboard 'Roly Roscoe' went back to Charleston.

Authors note. *Howard McGhee was a leading exponent of be-bop but addiction had taken its' toll. He was making a comeback in 1964. Phineas Newborn was a good choice having worked with B.B. King.*

Reuben was now alone in a prison cell in Jackson Mississippi, the last place on earth he wanted to be. Tales of police brutality, and even murder were not unknown and he knew he had to get out of there fast.

Sure a lawyer was provided, but Reuben had only one thing on his mind. In the morning he'd call Jed and Gina and ask them to help him again.

Once more the call came out of the blue as far as they were concerned. Perhaps optimistically they had thought that Reuben and his 'troubles' were over but they listened sympathetically on the 'speaker phone' while he outlined his latest crisis. Yes he was in prison on 'suspicion' of murder again, he told them, but it was another put-up job, he was convinced of it. Start with Roscoe he had said,' there's something not right about him.' He admitted that he had been in Vicksburg on the night of the murders but so had everyone else on the Muddy Waters tour. He also confessed that he had been drinking and had 'maybe' snorted some 'coke' but nothing like before, he said. He was back in his room by midnight he said but no, there were no witnesses to prove it. He'd got the impression that nobody was talking. It was well known that the 'Klan' operated locally, putting fear into the community and with fingers in nearly every pie including law enforcement. This being so, the Federal Government had soon sent in the FBI to investigate these 'cross state' murder charges.

According to Reuben they wanted a quick 'result and he was the 'patsy,' but he could do nothing to clear his name from inside his cell. Please come he had implored them, and of course they were on the next plane.

SOS. Jed&Gina arrive.

On arrival they booked into the same hotel that the 'Muddy' tour had occupied, hoping to pick up a few clues, or perhaps some indiscretions from staff gossip, but first they interviewed Reuben in his cell. This was allowed although the State had provided a defence lawyer, but it didn't take Jed and Gina long to see that he seemed to agree with the local police on nearly every point. The FBI insisted on being present also, deeming that Reuben was a flight risk and they did not want to risk plans being made to organise an escape. 'Nothing personal.' they said. So it was, that Jed and Gina returned to the hotel with very little to go on.

'We need to make a plan.' said Gina, 'and we might not have much time.

Let's take it from the beginning of the tour. Where did they go and how come they were in Vicksburg on the night of the murders? If it was a member of the troupe this would have had to be organised way back, but that's not possible because the Civil Rights people arrived well after the tour started. So it does seem that the presence of the Tour on that day was used by the real murderers to cast a smokescreen over their involvement.'

Jed was looking impressed, 'Yes that's all correct,' he said, 'but who are these people specifically when so many folk here in Mississippi appear to be fellow travellers of the Klan? That's got to be our starting point.' Gina nodded but then hesitated. 'I've got an idea.' she said. 'Do you remember when Reuben's keyboard player got into a fight and had to be replaced? Well apparently that was right out of character Reuben said. In fact he was suspicious of Roscoe from the start and I'm wondering, just wondering mind, if the fight was fixed so that a 'mole' could be planted in the middle of the tour entourage. I don't know why but it does seem possible, so I think we should try to find out a bit more about Mr Roscoe don't you? Perhaps he was just monitoring the group when he saw a real opportunity to cause racial mayhem. '<u>Black musician slays Peace Loving</u> <u>White Civil Rights Men.</u>' I can see it now, and it could still work.'

<u>Oh Mr Porter</u>

The next morning Gina made it her business to talk to some of the waitresses and chamber-maids. 'I know what it's like,' she would say, 'You're lucky if you get a smile let alone a tip.' This had led to some success in the past but not this time. Jed was luckier as he found the Night Porter in a mood to talk about the strange 'goings on' in Room 404.

'I remember it well,' the Porter began, 'Mr Roscoe told me that he was expecting visitors after midnight and that I was to bring them up to his room immediately. There would be a Mr Rainier and a Mr Simpson followed some time later by about another nine men arriving separately. I was to bring them all up and I did. I recognised some of them too. There was a well-known banker, a politician, a church leader (in dark black and a dog collar) and men carrying diplomatic or military bags. I don't miss much I can tell you. Later they called for a buffet and drinks and finally they left at 4.30 am. I know the precise time because Mr Roscoe called me from the room and asked me to clear it of all signs of a meeting before the chambermaids arrived in the morning. I agreed and when I got there he placed a $100 bill in my hand. 'No traces mind,' he said, 'leave it just as it was this morning. OK?' I said yes and started the clean up while he retired to his bedroom for a 'lie down' he said, but I heard a girl squealing. None of my business I thought unless it was something I might use against him later on, that is if I needed to. You have to look out for these things you know, maybe if they complain about service for example. One might say, 'And what was the service like last night Sir might I ask?' They usually detected a hidden threat and backed off then.

Well in this case it was a whole different ballgame. I'd never seen anything like it because Mr Roscoe had managed to move four large easels from the Conference Suite and they were set up in the four corners of the room. He was otherwise engaged so I took my time looking at each one in turn to see if there was anything interesting or maybe 'useful' as a bargaining chip later. To be honest though, none of it made sense to me. Let me explain. The easels were consecutively numbered H1, H2, H3 & H4 and it seemed likely that there had been a presentation to the guests in the room that night. Anyway I've learnt to be 'creative' in my line of work so I decided to keep all the paperwork, from the charts on the easels to the last scrap that had been thrown on the floor or put in the bin. I returned the easels to the Conference Suite and now here you are showing an interest. Maybe you can tell me how much interest.' he said with a grin.

Gina looked at Jed in disbelief. Could they have come across a major planning meeting of the mysterious organisation that they had been tracking for so many years? The very name Simpson had alerted them to this possibility and together with Reuben's suspicions about Roscoe they hardly dared to hope too much. Jed remembered how signatories on document found previously had sometimes contained the signatories, 'S' or 'H' or 'R' and that could tie in as well. Gina was beside herself with excitement but tried to hide it as Jed spoke first. 'Yes I suppose that we would like to see the papers but there may be absolutely nothing in them of course. If you bring them along I might make you an offer, maybe another $100 if there's something of interest.' Now the porter seemed offended. 'Madam seems very keen don't you think Sir?' he stated, smiling rather craftily, 'so before we proceed I think it best that we lay our cards on the table don't you? I know who you are from the Hotel register of course but I have a name too. I'm so sorry but I've just realised that I haven't introduced myself. Josef Luge at your pleasure, German origin you know but my best friends call me 'Scrooge' to rhyme with Luge. Yes, actually I'm quite good with money, getting it and keeping it you know, so now let's start again shall we? I'm thinking 4 figures not 3.'

The pair were taken aback by this development, but they knew that Luge held all the cards. 'Right Mr Luge' said Jed now rather frostily, 'Let's call it $500, that is if any of it is useful.' He held out his hand as if to seal the deal but once more Mr Luge smiled benignly. 'I don't think that I've made myself clear,' he said. 'I have a certain way of doing business. I never negotiate, I set the terms and on this occasion I have to tell you that you have made a big mistake in offering me such a paltry sum.' He seemed genuinely offended but continued. 'I said 4 figures and I meant it but now the price has gone up. For every discount that you try to secure I will add the same amount on top of the original sum. The price therefore is now $1500. Take it or leave it. It's a one time only offer'

They had been outfoxed, their planned holiday to Europe was now a pipe dream, they just had to accept, and Jed did so with all the grace that he could muster against this cunning little man. 'Very good Mr Luge, $1500 it is. If you bring everything here tomorrow morning I'll have the cash for you. OK?' 'I agree, it's such a pleasure to do business with you,' replied Mr Luge, 'thank you and good night.'

He was gone and Jed looked at Gina with a mixture of expectation and despair. Had they been fooled or was this really the 'silver lining' that they had dreamt of for so long?' She held out her arms and he slid gratefully into them nuzzling her warm breasts with a sigh.

The 'Crock of Gold'

The next day Jed and Gina began to investigate the heap of paperwork that Luge had left them, and they were not disappointed. Here, before their very eyes were the Foundation blocks, the Development of, and the Future of that elusive group seeking white supremacy in the 'Anglo Saxon' homelands that they had tracked for so long. Now they could give it a name. '**We are Hydra**' it declared brazenly on the flip charts that had adorned the easels in Room 404, each one with a different subtitle

H1 was simply entitled 'Hydra' and contained a list of formative dates and events since it's foundation in Revolutionary France.

H2 was entitled 'Angletown' and showed a similar development in the United States during and after the Civil War there.

H3 was entitled 'Saxonville' and once more listed, one might say, a creeping penetration of towns and cities throughout the world including the abortive support of Nazi Germany.

H4 was entitled 'Waterfall 1st January 1964' The page then explained that future plans were highly confidential at present but would be revealed.

Authors note. HI and H2 now presented the details given in the 'Hydra' chapter when Jed and Gina saw (or didn't see) the film. H3 details have been spread throughout the story from the start. H4 details are to come.

It seemed that the boards were telling a story. A tale of humble beginnings from which a worldwide organisation committed to the realisation of white racial purity in the 'Anglo Saxon' homelands was being realised. It also appeared to be a 'hard sell' to the guests who had been invited to the meeting, almost a 'take it or leave it' scenario in which they were invited to participate but 'marked' if they did not.

Now Jed and Gina had a task on their hands, namely to rummage through the many pieces of paper left behind. They needed clues so that they could learn more about Hydra and it's intentions.

The first sheet that they found was indeed most useful, appearing to be a backup (R/S eyes only, Rainier/Simpson?) to the H4 document. Simply put it stated that on 1st January 1964 Operation Waterfall would begin and all world communications networks would be immobilised. Following this, the nine appointed 'Heads' of Hydra would take immediate authority in their designated area. This would be possible because sympathetic and powerful leaders were already committed to the cause as were the Generals in NATO and other military set ups. A Supra-National Authority would be immediately established and a manifesto of aims and objectives issued. Referenda would be held 'in due time' when the benefits of the new world order had begun to be realised. It finished 'This land is ours. This land is not theirs. This is our future together.'

Jed and Gina were amazed at the effrontery and confidence shown in the document but they knew that it was all too serious. These plans had been in the making for more than a century and now Hydra was ready to strike.

They knew therefore that they must trawl through the remaining bag of paper, not only to find out more about the past but more importantly, the future. If a plan was already in place and sophisticated 'jamming' equipment ready to operate, where was it and could they find out in time?

There was only one thing for it and it began like an important civil ceremony. Jed picked up one corner of the large black bag and Gina picked up the other. Together they carried it to the middle of the room and, in a simultaneous gesture, cast its' contents to the floor. Always prepared to see the funny side of things, Jed made a short speech, 'Cast up your secrets deadly Hydra, your nine heads will not avail you now.' he said to polite and, it must be said, muted applause from Gina.

The bag contained the usual rubbish left over from a buffet supper in a hotel room but, once that was disposed of, they began to sort out the papers. Some documents were just folded, as the one that Gina had already found, but others were torn up in scattered pieces or screwed up into balls, some quite loosely and others very tightly as if to prevent any confidential details leaking out. While Jed had already begun to piece together the tiny scraps of paper that had spilled out, Gina sat thinking and Jed noticed that she wasn't taking part. 'What's up Gina?' he said, 'Don't know where to start?' In reply she pursed her lips and pointed, not to Jed's scraps or the neat folded A4 sheets in the opposite corner, but to the pile of screwed up paper that they had placed in a heap, looking a little like a 'papier mache' Mount Everest. 'See there,' she said as she pointed, 'the smaller balls seem to be on the top and the larger ones underneath. Now what is the purpose of climbing a mountain I ask you? Well, to get to the top of course and it's my hunch that our 'crock of gold' lies there, at the top. So this is my theory, small screwed up paper means top secret, folded means dummy run discard, and torn means useless under any circumstances. What do you think?' Jed couldn't help himself bursting into peals of laughter, he laughed so much that it hurt while Gina looked on. 'We are not amused.' she said and of course this set him off again. 'Oh Gina. Gina, I do love you so' he said 'but that's the daftest idea that I've heard for ages. You can't be serious can you?' Now she looked at him in mock disapproval and said, 'Let's see who's right then 'Dick Tracey'. I'll have my balls (forgive the pun) and you can have your itty-bitty jigsaw paper. Let's see who finds the 'treasure' first.' It was true enough that Jed had the worst of this bargain as he struggled to make sense of the small pieces, much as an archaeologist might do with hieroglyphics. Now it was his turn to cause amusement, 'I feel the power of Tutenkhamun.' he said, and Gina could not resist a smile. It was a long and arduous process and neither of them had anything to show for their endeavours after three hours. It was time to call a halt, Gina decided because she had another plan. 'Not another one.' said Jed with a smile.

'You always need a Plan B,' said Gina, 'just hear me out, it's connections we need isn't it? So let's look for names, place names or any names, then, from that particular document, find another reference point. Let's say that 'Boston' is paired with, say, 'Simpson,' but on another document, 'Boston' is paired with 'Hydra,' do you see, that could link 'Simpson' to 'Hydra' although it would need another source to verify the assertion.'

Jed nodded, 'Yes, let's do it' he said grinning, 'after all it's your best idea so far.' Gina turned away in a mock huff but soon she turned back in triumph. 'Eureka' she shouted out loud, 'I've got it' and then, rather quieter, 'well I've got something to make a start. Come and look. See, here on this piece it says 'Waterfall,' the operation's code name but look, there, it's the beginning of another word ripped off, it looks like 'Doubt.'

Maybe they're not sure about the date, but I found another piece that says 'Date confirmed' signed R (for Rainier). What do you make of that?'

'I suppose there could be some doubts,' said Jed, 'but look, I've got a strange one as well. This piece is very small but you can see that it says 'lans for engineering at

Hydr . . .' and there the piece is torn. Well obviously it means Plans but why would Hydra need engineering?' 'Mmm, let me see,' said Gina, carefully holding the tiny piece in her hand, 'I can't quite make it out but the tear seems to be in the middle of an O not an A. Look at the shape, that makes it Hydro not Hydra. Well done Jed, I think we're getting somewhere. We're looking for a Hydro Electric Dam, I don't know why or where but we sure are. And another thing, remember the operation codeword, yes, 'Waterfall' isn't it?'

'I can add a bit more,' said Jed, 'I've noticed the word 'South' cropping up quite a lot, but nothing about North, East or West. Now what do you make of that?' Gina responded at once as if she wished that she had said it first, 'I've found quite a few of those as well,' she said, 'meaning?'

'Can't be sure,' said Jed, 'but this bit fits in with the notion of jamming the world's networks. It says 'Sound confirmed,' probably the result of some trial run. Let's keep looking.' Another hour passed before they sat wearily in the corner of the room to compare notes. 'I've found this one,' said Jed, 'it's on Simpson Line notepaper and, as you would expect, it seems to be about shipping, itineraries, cargo etc but it's only page one of two and finishes, 'Details of funnel widening are enclosed for your . . .'

Now what sense does that make?' 'Simple.' Said Gina, 'It's tunnels not funnels, maybe a typo but that fits in nicely with our scenario so far doesn't it? A Hydro Electric Dam that needs tunnels, powered by a waterfall somewhere in the 'South.' 'Right,' said Jed, 'Well, for a start I'm going to narrow down that 'South' angle. Let's be logical now. The word South could only mean 3 things in geographical terms I think, namely the South Pole, the South Pacific or South America, none of which fit an Anglo Saxon profile or our terrain for the dam. However I have another one up my sleeve because I have a cousin who lives there. It fits the bill in every way. It's the 'South' Island of New Zealand.' Gina could not contain her excitement once more. 'That's it Jed, you are wonderful. All the pieces are beginning to fit. We had 'doubt, sound, tunnels and south.' Obvious isn't it? Hydra's lair is in 'Doubtful Sound,' that isolated fiord region to the south of South Island New Zealand.'

Their work was done and they flopped happily onto the piles of paper.

With all this excitement they had quite forgotten about Reuben still languishing in a Charleston cell. Fortunately his 'dubious' lawyer called them later that very day to say that he had been released without charge. He joined them the next day and was pleased to hear of their progress. However he did not agree with Jed's proposal that they contact the Highlander group again. 'Firstly' he said, 'remember that I was a mole in their midst when I was on drugs, and secondly they're just too big to be sure that everyone is reliable, and anyway I've got something to say.'

This sounded ominous and Jed and Gina waited for any new 'Reuben revelation' that he was about to tell them. Nothing would be a surprise or would it? They waited as Reuben stood up and began with these words.

Dear friends. Dear Gina and Dear Jed. You have done so much for me and for us, the Solidar family, and I want to say thank you. But that's not enough. I want to do something positive now. If you plan to go to New Zealand I'm coming with you. 'All for all and all for one,' remember?'

If Doubtful Sound is the Hydra's lair I want to be there when we find it.

He sat down, there was no applause, just a stunned silence, and then Jed and Gina got up, walked across and held him warmly. They were only too aware of the dangers to come but all realised that they must see it through, until that sinister plot had been exposed and destroyed for good.

THE HYDRA'S LAIR

The 'Three Musketeers' were as certain as they could be that the Hydra communication centre lay in Doubtful Sound. The Sound itself lies in the province of Otago on the South West coast of the South Island in New Zealand at the heart of the Fiordland National Park. Otago itself was heavily settled by European migrants mostly from the UK and especially during the Gold Rush of the 1880's. The Maori named the newcomers 'Pakeha'; wars were fought and peace made but some antipathies still remain over rights to the foreshore etc.

Authors note. *I apologise if there are a few chronological inaccuracies in this story. Maybe the National Park came later but the terrain is still the same, it's remoteness and ruggedness appreciated by many visitors. Films such as the recent Lord of the Rings trilogy have been made here.*

The region is beautiful yet bacchanalian. It is secret and sinister as well as stunning as the mists roll in, and it was here that the trio were headed without quite knowing what to expect or what dangers might lie ahead.

An international flight took them to Wellington the NZ capital and soon after arrival they transferred onto a local flight to Queenstown, the regional centre. The town has been built along the shores of Lake Wakatipu and is under the protection of the Coronet Peak Ski area. The steamship SS Earnshaw still plies its' trade up and down the lake and sheep fuel the local economy. Gold was a big inducement to immigrants during the 1880's Gold Rush when many Scots families arrived to try their luck in places like Arrowtown. Scots town names remain, as in Invercargill and Dunedin so, not unnaturally it was a Scots sea captain known only as 'Cap'n Bob' who took them up Doubtful Sound in the motor vessel Tutoka III after a two-hour drive from Queenstown.

Once in the Sound itself Cap'n Bob ordered silence so that seals and dolphins would feel confident enough to come out and play. Gina was spellbound and might have forgotten why she was there in the first place had it not been for Jed disturbing her reverie with a whisper. 'Back there' he said, 'Look, the Hydra's lair.' She could only respond with a brief 'Shsh.' as she watched two dolphins approach the boat and seem to stand up for any fish titbits that might come their way. No luck there because the reserve forbids any feeding of the wildlife so that the proper ecology will be maintained. Soon they disappeared beneath the still surface of the Lake and then Gina did look back.

Yes, there it was, shrouded in mist, partly because of the ambient temperature in the Sound itself but also because of the spray caused by the waterfall that drove the power station. She shivered. It had become chilly but this was more a tremor of uncertainty, one might almost say, fear as she huddled herself against Jed. She knew that soon, very soon, they would be off the boat and on a coach headed for the far side of the foothills, thence to drive a whole two kilometres inside a single tunnel wherein lay the Manapouri Lake Power Station. There they would find Station guides and take part in a brief tour and it was there that she, and the others hoped to find evidence of Hydra. The approach was scary enough as the coach negotiated tight bends in the solid granite tunnel, but a different kind of anxiety took over when it turned into a large well-lit underground hall with purring machines at every corner. Indeed was this going to be a complete wild goose chase? There just seemed to be nothing unusual and Gina could see that Jed was looking anxious. This had been her idea hadn't it so what if they found nothing? She didn't dare to think of what that might mean as they all tried to act normally, and tried not to ask too many leading questions from the very helpful guides who were showing many different parties of tourists around. It was Reuben who broke the ice as he stood close to a large map of the Power Station. 'Come here you two,' he said, as he had done before, 'See, here, see these doors, big doors at both ends of this hall. Do you think there's anything strange about them?' Jed looked at Gina and she looked back rather blankly. 'Not really,' said Jed, 'everything that we can see is on the map isn't it? Look, Transformer Number One, there it is over there, and there it is on the map.' 'Exactly Jed, you said it yourself.' replied Reuben. 'You said 'everything that we can see' but what about what we can't see? What's behind those doors for instance? And another thing, have you noticed how the 'guides' by those doors are wearing a different uniform? It's blue not grey, the badge is H for Hydra maybe not MPS, for Manapouri Power Station and look, who needs a Kalashnikov down here? They seem to, because they are guarding the Lair. That's why.'

Jed looked at Gina in disbelief, and she looked at him with some relief. 'How come I missed all that,' thought Jed and, it must be admitted, Gina was thinking the same thing. Obviously they did not want to draw attention to themselves at this stage so a small pat on the back would have to suffice for now. Not exactly the NAACP badge awarded to Reuben Senior, but surely at least its' equivalent, awarded two miles inside a granite mountain 3000 miles from home.

Back at the hotel there were more fulsome praises and a glass or two but Jed still needed to remind the other two that they were far from proving anything. In fact they hadn't really 'found' anything either. 'I hate to say it,' he said, 'but we're going to need some help after all. Now that we're here in New Zealand I don't think we can look back to the States with Highlander for example. No, we need something local but also International in it's reach.' 'And trustworthy.' added Gina, 'and that's all a tall order.' Reuben was looking dejected, 'I say we go back and hide out until we can get a better look,' he said, 'We can't give up now.' Jed took his arm affectionately, 'No Reuben, you know we won't but we've got to be reasonable and adopt a plan that stands some chance of success don't you agree?' Reuben nodded in the affirmative and Gina did the same.

'Whom do you have in mind to help then Jed?' she asked. 'CND that's who.' he said, 'I took the liberty of doing some research back home in case we came to this impasse. They have a formal wing of course but there are others, on the periphery of the group who have been and are prepared to take on more risky ventures. There's a guy called Josh Middleton who is resident here in NZ. I suggest we set up a meeting.'

Authors note. *CND had been very active in the South Pacific from 1961, and in 1962 they petitioned the NZ government to oppose French A bomb tests in Polynesia. As stated, they tended to follow a legalistic line in normal circumstances, unlike Greenpeace whose ship 'Rainbow Warrior' was sunk 'by the French' in Auckland Harbour in 1985.*

The others agreed that they should all to meet up with Josh as soon as possible. Fortunately he said that he could meet them at the 'Wrinkly Rams' wine bar the next day 'no strings attached.' This caveat was in their minds also as Jed gave him an outline of their suspicions. However he soon put their minds at rest as he explained. 'My group over here is tiny and we have the advantage of operating within the CND umbrella, but naturally we have a great deal of autonomy, given the distance. We are nine actually, which is a bit of a coincidence given your notions about Hydra, the nine headed beast now in Doubtful Sound. To be truthful we have had our eye on the Manapouri Power station for some time, maybe for different reasons but some of us believe that it's a lot more than it seems to be, and if what you've told me turns out to be true, it's vital that we accelerate our plans to gain entry.' He smiled, 'Yes, we do have such a plan but it's not without great risk. You see the only real prospect of getting in unnoticed is by mountain ladders up the face of the waterfall.'

Gina's face dropped, Reuben stated fidgeting and Jed seemed shocked but pulled himself together at once. 'That's terrific Josh,' he said, 'When do we start?'

Josh laughed. 'Sorry Jed, you've done your bit. This next phase needs experienced mountaineers. We are, and we're always practising up in the 'Remarkables' or up in the 'Coronet Peaks.'

Jed looked at the others, 'No deal,' he said, 'we're going with you and if we need some training we'll get it within the next few weeks. End of story.' Jed could see that, apprehensive though they might be, the other two were squarely behind him as they both nodded vigorously. Josh held up his hands in a gesture of surrender and said, 'Right, that's that then, I'll get some training sorted right away and then we'll discuss who does what on the night, Agreed?' It was, and training began in earnest.

Their instructor was to be a formidable, one might even say fearsome Maori called 'Tamaki,' and the first item on his agenda was to show them what they were up against. He'd found a spot, he said, that was similar but perhaps not so big as Manapouri but what it lacked in size it made up in terms of danger. A few miles from Queenstown, up and past the 'Edith Cavell' bridge and into 'Skippers' Canyon' there was a ravine just named 'Death' he said, because so many would be mountaineers had perished there. 'Safe in Tamakis' hands.' he said very seriously, 'but not yet. You must learn how to use the equipment and the hand signals that may keep you from danger. We'll now go back to my small farm and practise until you are ready to climb 'Death' without difficulty.' Once more he sounded so serious in a situation which seemed so surreal and 'out of this world' to Gina' that she had to try really hard to suppress a laugh. 'Climb death without difficulty' she repeated and nearly burst into song. However one look at Tamaki soon convinced her otherwise.

The lesson began and they soon became familiar with their 'tools of the trade.' Rope, 11mm Edelrid LSK and 12mm E Braid Capstan, Oval steel Screwgate Petzl Head torch, Crampons and a selection of short rope ladders known as 'etriers' or 'aiders.' In addition there was a variety of robust climbing jackets, trousers and boots. All these had to be tried and then used, experimentally against a large barn door, not without mishap unfortunately because a heavy fall caused Reuben to abandon any hope of the climb due to a twisted ankle. 'But you can't stop me from coming.' he said, 'You'll definitely need someone at the base and that'll be me.'

Next Tamaki stressed how important it was that they knew about climbing calls. 'There must be no misunderstandings once you begin to ascend and descend.' he said, and then went through some fairly obvious ones such as' OK', 'Climb on', and 'Safe' but added many more that he told them to learn because they might save lives. 'Below' was a good example, a warning that something has been dislodged, or 'Slack' meaning that a rope is too tight and might snap. He told them about rappelling, belaying and abseiling and Jed and Gina soon began to feel confident with Tamaki at their side, less so when he told them that he would not be there. 'Ancient Spirits on the Lake.' he said, 'No wild horse would persuade me to go. Sorry.' So there it was, they would have to depend on themselves and others of course. However that was not the end of the bad news. Josh had decided to send two teams up the face, one on the East side and the other on the West. 'We know that there are vast doors on either side of the main hall so one team will investigate the East and the other the West and from what you've told me already,' he said, 'I know that you both have a vast amount of data on Hydra so I can't afford to lose you both if something goes wrong with one of the teams. So you'll have to separate, you in Team A, Gina, and you Jed, in Team B with me. Team A will be led by our best mountaineer Gino Belluno who comes from a leading Alpine mountaineering family in the Dolomites.' Noticing that they both looked worried he just said, 'And that's final.'

The Lair Itself

The first thing was to set up a base camp about half a mile from the falls. It was then agreed that there should be a 'recce' before the climb itself just to view the base of the waterfall, and to spot any barriers should they be natural or man made. Jed and Gina did not go nor Reuben, who was still recovering from his fall, so Josh led a small team of four in a 'kayak' canoe. Time seemed to drag as the others waited for their return but soon enough they were back, and Josh was looking very serious. No one wanted to speak first as the team all came in and huddled together in the damp air. 'Pass me our Naval Directory please Mike.' he said to one of the group that had stayed behind. Mike went to a small bookcase and took a large blue bound volume that looked like 'Janes Shipping Guide' but Jed could see that the cover contained the initials, 'RN' for Royal Navy. Josh opened the book carefully, read for a few moments and then put it down. 'As I thought,' he said, 'there's a submarine down there and not just any old sub. I've done the measurements and I can tell you exactly what it is and what it can do.' This was the last thing that any of them had expected and it was to get worse. Josh continued in a rather matter of fact manner as if reporting a new car at the 'Earls Court' motor show. 'British Nuclear Submarine Resolution.' he began, 'Length 425, Beam 33, 7.5 tons, 33 knots, 150 crew. Armed with16 Polaris missiles, 6 Torpedo Tiger Fish and sub harpoon anti ship missiles. Obsolete from Royal Navy and thought to have been scrapped along with Renown. Repulse and Revenge.' He stopped, 'Now we're in real trouble,' he said, 'there's bound to be maximum security so does anyone want to back out? It's a different ballgame now.' The room remained silent and, if anything, faces now took on a more determined look. 'Count us in.' said Jed.

It was two days later when the two teams set out for the cliffs and the waterfall. Fortunately there was a misty moonlight that allowed them to see but hopefully not to be seen as they approached the shore-line. Gina looked up as the water cascaded down into the Lake. She couldn't even see the top but soon Gino had his team organised, 'Avanti! Let's go.' he said and began the climb. Tamaki had taught her well and soon Gina and the others were not far behind. Perhaps she should not have looked down because, as she did so, the world went dizzy and she dropped a climbing hammer. She looked at Gino but he signalled 'No,' meaning no 'Below' call to those following. It was too risky to make a sound, and hopefully they could see it coming and take evasive action. There were no more incidents, and soon they reached a small plateau between the rock face and the large building that they had entered from the other side through the 2km tunnel. They approached the windows carefully but could see little, probably due to years of weathering in that hostile place. Gina didn't know what she had expected but this was a real disappointment.

'So near, and yet so far' she thought as Gino shrugged rather helplessly.

Josh had led his team, including Jed, to the top without incident but once there they faced the same dilemma. Of course they did not know how the other team was doing, but according to their pre-planning both teams were due back on the kayaks in 45 minutes. The team skirted the building and at last found a large sewage pipe that pointed out to the Lake. Josh was not dismayed, 'I was expecting something like this. Here.' he said opening his Rucksack and taking out 3 gasmasks. 'All I could lay my hands on. They're probably First World War so I hope they still work.'

This he said with a smile and went on, 'Neville, Jed and me, we'll go in. Others wait here and if we're not back on time, leave. That's an order.'

Unfortunately, barely had the three begun their journey along the dark passage before Neville suddenly collapsed in a heap gasping for breath and Josh and Jed had to carry him back to the waiting group. Josh had said that the gasmasks were old but he had expected them to work. There were obviously more noxious elements in the tunnel than just sewage and he felt he should make sure that Jed still wanted to go on. A nod was sufficient and they started again, now with only 35 minutes to go. They soon found a hatch that took them into a sort of washroom adjoining a suite of offices that seemed to be unoccupied. They could see a guard on the other side of a frosted glass door but much of the room was obscured from his vision. 'Right.' said Josh, 'you know what you're looking for. Just be quick about it.' It wasn't easy. Jed wanted to take every document that he came across but after about 10 minutes he had made a selection. They would have to hope that the papers would not be missed for some time, that is before the premises could be raided by some official law enforcement officers. Slipping the papers into a waterproof bag they began their journey back, just in time but there was not much joy at their return. Jed could see a black plastic cover over a body and feared the worst. 'Neville didn't make it.' said one, 'we couldn't save him. Sorry.' There was a stunned silence as Josh gathered his thoughts, 'Well,' he said, 'he's coming home with us. Come on let's make a trestle.' In this manner they descended the cliff and met up with the other team. Nothing much was said as they drifted out silently into that 'Doubtful Sound' that had claimed another victim. They could not afford to stay at base camp in case their presence had been detected, so after awhile they picked up a launch at a pre-planned place and headed for home. 'Home' were the Luxury Lakeside Spinnaker Bay Apartments heading out of Queenstown on the Frankton road. They had taken all of the 16 luxury suites for security reasons as much as anything else, but there was a sombre mood when they returned late that night. Over dinner Josh made a short thank you speech and ended with these words, 'Let's raise our glasses to our own hero, Neville Barton and make sure that his death was not in vain'.

There was muted excitement the next day as Jed carefully unwrapped his 'hoard' taking each document carefully and handing them to Gina who had set up a sort of 'category' display on the floor. Yes, there she was again, trying to make sense of this complex case just as she had done before with her Pepper pots and fruit, but now they were closing in or were they? To be blunt there were references to a group called 'Hydra,' even a brief history together with lists of names and letters to and fro, but as to a worldwide conspiracy, Jed put it simply, 'I'm afraid that we're drawing a blank.' he said. Gina wanted to cry and Reuben was all for going back and getting more evidence so it was fortunate that Josh saw the thing from a completely different perspective. 'Nil desperandum,' he said with that big grin of his, 'we wouldn't be here if it wasn't for you three and we owe you a lot but this case reminds me a little of the FBI case against Al Capone, incarcerated for tax evasion, not murder, robbery or trafficking. No, the authorities couldn't make that stick but he was put away for years and his 'Empire' broken up. That's what we all want at the end of the day isn't it? So what is our 'tax evasion' angle?' he said and then paused, a little like a comedian waiting for the right moment to deliver his punch line. Sure he milked his audience, looking around the room back and forth with a confident smile before he continued.

'Resolution' that's what,' he said, 'what self-respecting government would allow a fully functioning nuclear submarine to be based in their territory? This is one area where the NZ Parliament will not listen to contrary advice from arguably 'greater' world powers. I can assure you that once they are informed there will be swift action with all the powers that the country possesses. There is no doubt that the site will be closed and those responsible captured and brought to trial. Case closed, end of Hydra. And by the way I propose to make another charge against the leadership, that of murder, or at least involuntary manslaughter for the way in which poisonous gases had not been contained on the site leading to the death of Neville Barton. I said that he would not have died in vain'

It turned out just as Josh had forecast. The NZ authorities threw every law enforcement and military power at their command against the fortress. They then threw every book possible at the Hydra leadership including Rainier and Simpson. By now the case was a 'cause celebre' in the world media, and other foreign governments soon came to recognise that no good could come from retaining links with a Hydra with no heads. It might be said then, that Jed and Gina's involvement with the Solidar family was a catalyst for change and that change is still going on.

Foot-note

Back in the States Jed and Gina soon got back to their rather more humdrum lives but they kept in touch with Reuben who now made his first LP. The title was 'A Doubtful Sound,' and some well-intentioned A&R man wrote these sleeve-notes.

'Reuben has that wistful muted sound reminiscent of Miles Davis epitomized in the expression that 'Miles walks on eggshells.' It is this vulnerability that Reuben seeks to address with his chosen title for this excellent piece of work. Obviously it also resonates with the title that John Coltrane gave his 1959 seminal LP 'A Love Supreme.'

Authors note. *Hah! We know different don't we? If Reuben had made the notes I'm sure it would have just said, 'With heartfelt thanks to my friends Jed and Gina and in loving memory of my uncle Reuben Solidar and my father Cecil Solidar.'*

END OF STORY

MUSICAL TIMELINE

Part One 1900-1942 (Didn't he ramble)

Jedsy Lomax gets more than he bargained for when he invites Cecil Solidar to tell the story of his brother Reuben (The Ghost). They were both jazz musicians starting out in New Orleans in 1900 and making their way via Chicago to New York with bigotry and racism ever present.

(RR denotes a Reuben 'ghost' recording.)

New Orleans 1900-22 (Mr Jelly Roll, Riverboats and the Mardis Gras)

Chicago 1923 King Oliver's Creole Jazzband

New York 1924-6 RR-Naughty Man (Henderson/Hawkins)

Chicago 1927 RR-Chicago Breakdown(Dickerson//Ory+)

New York 1928-33 (Great Depression, Mafia and the 'Lindy Hop')

1929 RR-Too Late (Oliver/ Frazier)

1932 Reuben's career and 'SS Observation' go up in flames.

Chicago1933 RR-Wrappin' it up (Henderson/clt/Smith*tpt)

European Tours, (Recordings and a Plastic Surgeon 1933-38) London(Roy Fox—*Paris* RR Dinah (Wells)-*Berlin* (Hylton)

New York 1938-40 All RR—Harlem shout (Lunceford/Thomas) *1938*

—Ghost of a chance (Calloway/ Berry) *1938*-Moonlight serenade (Miller/clt Shwartz/ tpt Erwin)—*1939* Solitude (Ellington /Webster) *1940*

Part Two 1943-53 (Sentimental Journey)

Reuben had been killed in a race row in 1942 so Jed joins forces with Gina and Cecil to unmask the culprits in the Swing era of the Big Bands, Jimmy Dorsey, Les Brown, Charlie Barnet, Claude Thornhill, Woody Herman, Count Basie and Lionel Hampton.

Part Three 1954-64 (Hurrah for Hollywood)

After the war Jed sets out to help Reuben Junior who has been arrested on dubious charges related to a famous Hollywood actress. In doing so he becomes aware of a sinister group known only as the 'Covenant.'

RR Peanut Vendor (Kenton) *1952*, Kalamazoo (<u>Miller **Film**</u>) *1953*

I want to live (<u>Mulligan **Film**</u>) *1958*. After you've gone (Goodman) *1962*

Part Four 1770-1870 (Hydra)

Music takes a back seat as we explore the origins of the group known as Hydra during revolutionary times.

Part Five 1964 (Reuben's revenge)

Reuben tours with Muddy Waters and Jed and Gina finally expose the Hydra's lair.

HISTORICAL TIMELINE

The Solidar brothers were respected as studio/jazz musicians for the best part of thirty years but those same years were ones of turmoil in America. Not only were there two world wars, but there was a continuous battle between criminal gangs (incl the Mafia,) and law enforcement, including the FBI. Alongside this conflict lay an even more insidious stream in American society, that of a rejection of 'liberal' ideas leading to a conflation of racial prejudice and anti-communism. Sooner or later people had to make a stand, some with the NAACP. It also soon becomes apparent that such dreams of white supremacy are not confined to the United States and indeed that there might well be a world conspiracy to achieve racist purity. When Reuben Jnr gets caught up in a scandal in Hollywood, Jed & Gina become aware of a group called **HYDRA**.

Part One (1900-42)

1900-22 NAACP 1909, '2nd' KKK 1915, World War One 1917-18, Prohibition 1919, 70 lynchings in 1919. race riots in Chicago, Parcel bombs, Wall St bomb kills 38 in 1920. IWW Trials & exec (1927)

1923 Oklahoma Governor expelled by KKK as they win seats.

1-6 Wm McAdoo KKK candidate loses to Davis for Democratic Presidential nomination. Progressive Party of la Follette fails.

1927 Lindbergh flight. He becomes hero but also suspect fascist.

1928-32 Wall Street Crash 1929. Riverboat explosion in New York 1932.

1933-4 Assassination of Huey Long and attempt on Roosevelt in Chicago. (wins in '36 &'44). Father Coughlin forms 'National Union of social justice' but it is anti Semitic. Am, Liberty league. (ALL) 1934.

1935-6 UAW (United Auto Workers formed.) Strike at GM Flint.

1933-39 Foreign affairs. Nazis elected in Germany (33) Abdication (36), Spanish Civil War (37) G occupy Austria, Czech, and Poland (39).

The Battle of Britain (1940), Pearl Harbour (Dec 1941), The 'Draft', Japan captures Singapore and Philippines. US ex order 9006 (Feb 42) removes all Japanese-Americans from California.

Part Two (1943-53)

Second world war comes to an end and Cold war begins.

Part Three (1954-64)

Novak scandal (54, Russian A bomb and Korean War, 'McCarthyism,' and anti-communism (Hollywood Ten). Civil Rights leaders (incl. Martin Luther King) are suspected of links with the 'Reds'. Civil Rights, Brown vs Topeka(54) Washington bus boycott (55) Bay of Pigs (61). Monroe 'suicide' (62), Cuba (62) JFK assassination (63.)

Part Four (1770-1870)

These dates go back a long way and come with apologies from the author who is only seeking to backtrack to a reasonable starting date for the parlous state of racial integration in the United States. Liberalism in Europe and elsewhere, as well as Slavery and the Civil War set the context because our story is about the Solidar family from New Orleans; but as we have already seen, there have been separate though connected developments in Europe, Africa and throughout the world.

(The creation of the group HYDRA is fictional.)

1770 US Declaration of Independence. 'That all men are created equal.'

1793 Haiti 'blood soaked insurrection' many slave owners killed.

1819 Slave state admitted to the north. (Missouri Compromise Line.)

1822 Inaugural meeting of HYDRA follows foundation of Monrovia by the 'American Colonisation Society', later Liberia. The objective is 'to rid the US of it's racially undesirable Afro-Americans.'

1827 The 'Anglo African Society' has the same intention.

1834 Slavery is abolished in the British Empire & 1848 in France.

1848 'Liberal' Revolutions in Europe & The Communist Manifesto.

The American Civil War

1854 The Kansas Nebraska Act said that settlers could decide slavery.

1856 Pro Slavers attack Lawrence. John Brown attacks Pottawattie.

1860 S. Carolina dissolves Union 'now subsisting' starts Confederacy.

VP Stephens states that 'The Negro is not equal to the white man.'

(Missississipi is second State to secede)

1861-3 The Civil War from Fort Sumter to Gettysburg.

1865 The End of the Civil War. Confederacy surrenders at Appamatox.

1865 President Lincoln is assassinated

1875 Mississippi 'Red Shirts' formed. (To drive blacks from the Polls)

(Curtin-African History, Von Drehle—Civil War, A. Cooke—America)

Part Five. 1964

1964 Civil Rights Act. Discrimination is outlawed and the Equal Opportunity Commission set up but activists are murdered in Mississipi.

Appendix
The role of the Church

Our story has contained references to the <u>Roman Catholic Church</u> before and after World War II. We reported that the American priest Father Coughlin, the founder of 'Hate Radio' was pronouncing <u>anti Semitic</u> propaganda in the 1930's and this was bad enough, but during the war, despite many reports of atrocities the Church did very little to speak out '<u>as an Institution</u>' although many brave Catholics and others did so, some dying as a result. Post war it was <u>Communism and Racism</u> that went hand in hand according to the bigots, and once more the Church was found wanting. Below are a few examples to demonstrate these points.

1   The Spanish Civil War. Vatican support for Fascist General Franco.

2   The Vatican's role in aiding Nazi leaders including Klaus Barbie.
     Vatican response is to admit to some errors of omission only.

3   The Vatican gave support to the clerical fascist (pro Nazi-anti Communist governments) in Croatia and Slovakia. Catholic 'storm troopers' (the Ustashi), were deployed in forced conversions, mass murders and in exterminations supervised by some Catholic clergy. (Source *The Vatican's Holocaust by Avro Manhattan.*)

4   The role of Pope Pius XIII as leader of the Catholic community.
     'He maintained a public front of indifference and remained silent while German atrocities were committed. He refused pleas for help on the grounds of neutrality in places as far apart as Poland, France, Italy, Switzerland, Romania, Greece and even Berlin in Germany.' Privately he may have sympathised but he did almost nothing in an official capacity and that was what was needed. (Source *Jewish Virtual Library*)

5   Centuries of Anti-Semitism in all Christian Churches allowed the growth of Nazism. Leading Nazis such as Julius Streicher were Christians, he himself a Catholic stating 'I follow Dr Martin Luther who wrote that 'The Jews are the serpent's brood and one should burn down their synagogues and destroy them.' (Source *Wikipedia*)

Conclusion.

In the novel we referred to a 'common cause' amongst those who believed in an 'Anglo Saxon' racial superiority, and to which other facets became attached such as anti-Semitism, anti-communism and racism. By seeming to be indifferent, and sometimes tacitly supportive of such excess, the 'Church' made the task of these racial demagogues in the real world and in our story much easier.